Theaker Quarterly Fiction #48

Edited by
Stephen Theaker
and John Greenwood

Other titles from this publisher and related entities

Theaker's Quarterly Fiction #48

Edited by
Stephen Theaker
and John Greenwood

Cover Artist

Howard Watts

Contributors

Tim Jeffreys
Tim Atkinson
Jacob Edwards
Howard Watts
Stephen Theaker
Charles Wilkinson
Douglas J. Ogurek
Antonella Coriander

ISBN (print): 978-1-910387-01-6

ISBN (epub): 978-1-910387-02-3

ISSN (print): 1747-6083

ISSN (online): 1747-6075

Website: www.theakersquarterly.blogspot.com

Email: theakersquarterlyfiction@gmail.com

Lulu Store: www.lulu.com/silveragebooks

Feedbooks: www.feedbooks.com/userbooks/tag/tqf

Submissions: Submissions are very welcome! See website for guidelines and terms.

Advertising: We welcome ad swaps with small press publishers and other creative types, and we'll run ads for relevant new projects from former contributors.

Sending material for review: We are interested in reviewing almost anything that's fantasy-related. We prefer to receive books for review in epub or mobi format. Feel free to send ebooks without querying first. We review about 10% of items received.

Mission statement: The primary goal of *Theaker's Quarterly Fiction* is to keep going. We need a new secondary goal.

Published in Theaker's Paperback Library on 25 August 2014.

Contents

Editorial

Fiction

The Quarterly Review

Reviews by Stephen Theaker, Jacob Edwards, Douglas J. Ogurek and Tim Atkinson

CONTENTS

Potatoes with Strong Views on Ketchup

Stephen Theaker

Christopher Priest, author of *The Prestige*, recently reviewed the book *Barricade* by Jon Wallace, and the review was not complimentary. Other reviews have been better, others even worse, but the Priest review really bothered some people, especially a few who had attended the book's launch party. They probably thought they were doing him a favour by fighting back against the review. What they really did was make sure everyone knew exactly how bad Christopher Priest thought the book was.

For one author, the problem was that Priest and Wallace share a publisher. He said that "The author that gives a scathing review of another author AT THE SAME PUBLISHER is a fucking idiot" (so you know how far to trust anything that writer says about books from his own publishers).

Perhaps that is sound advice for newbies climbing their way up the pole, trying to make friends, and wanting to keep a publisher sweet. But it's hardly likely to carry weight with a writer and critic who has been in the business for going on half a century.

For me, it's the word "scathing" in that sentence that makes it seem so rotten.

Another author put forward the idea that reviewers should follow the advice of his Great Aunt Daph: "If you can't say anything nice, don't say anything." Is that really what we want from reviewers? When you look up a hotel on TripAdvisor, do you want the reviewers to ignore the cockroaches and the all-night disco? When you're buying a washing machine, are you annoyed by reviewers who mention how hard it is to load and how often it breaks down?

Of course not, and why should books be any different? Maybe in that books are produced by writers, and reviews are produced by writers, so authors feel we should be on their side. Or maybe it's that books are cheap, so if money is wasted on bad ones, at least it's not a lot of money. Or that publishing itself is on the ropes, and needs our unquestioning support.

I don't agree. If we all agree that books are important, it's important to help readers find the good ones. Money is tight for everyone, not just publishers and authors. When I post reviews on Amazon, it's usually to make sure fellow customers don't spend their money without knowing about the problems with a product, and that goes for books as much as washing machines.

For example, a one volume edition of Baum's Oz books had removed all paragraph breaks to fit them in, turning every chapter into one enormous paragraph. The *Little Book of Hindu Deities* was lovely, but fell apart in a week because of poor binding. And several SF Gateway books were published without the scanning being checked, and thus have serious errors throughout. No conscientious reviewer could fail to mention such serious flaws.

If I'm wrong and reviewers should indeed look to our aunts for advice, let's talk about mine, who as a young girl in Plymouth put pieces of dried-up white dog poop into bags and told other children it was popcorn. If you were in a queue to eat that "popcorn", who would you want reviewing it, Great Aunt Daph or Christopher Priest?

I can understand why someone might read a review, especially of a book by someone that they know, and dislike it, think it too harsh, inaccurate, whatever. That happens all the time. I've yet to read a review of Adam Sandler's *Jack and Jill* with which I agree, and I suspect I never will. And if you spend more than an hour in my company there's a good chance of hearing me grumble about that.

But people didn't just grumble about Priest's review, they were furious with it. It showed "vile, condescending smugness", and was "predatory", "pompous", "ruthless", even "bullying". Personally, I think it was positively unhealthy how many writers encouraged the reviewed author to see himself as having been bullied by Priest.

Yes, some of them had just been to the book's launch party, and share the same publisher, and that may have led to them being a bit over-protective and coming on a bit too strong, but if someone plans to spend a lifetime writing books, and thus a lifetime receiving reviews, he would be better advised to take bad reviews a bit less personally than that.

Some thought it went even further than bullying: "It's one thing to beat a kid up on his (or her) first day at school, it's quite another to carve your name into their forehead with a straight-edge razor." Comparing a bad review to bullying is daft enough, but to compare it to a razor blade to the face shows a stunning lack of perspective. It's a review, a piece of writing where someone says whether they like a book or not and why. Even with the most vitriolic, spite-fuelled reviews you get out there, authors can just shrug and say, that's what they think.

Ironically, the author who said that was reading at the Super Relaxed Fantasy Club in London. Surely,

being relaxed about fantasy has to include being cool
with negative reviews.

The writer of the razor-blade comment went on to
say, "I don't see why delivering a balanced review in a
neutral voice is so difficult". But what does balance
mean in this context, and why is a neutral voice so
desirable? Would a neutral voice have made
Christopher Priest's review a better piece of writing?
More interesting? More amusing? Do we want him to
pretend that the review was not written by
Christopher Priest? Surely not – the whole approach of
the review was that of an older writer offering
avuncular advice to the younger.

Regarding balance, I try to follow Peter Tennant's
advice: to allocate space in a review proportionately.
Balance doesn't mean listing an equal number of good
points and bad points, it means not ignoring the good,
not ignoring the bad. If there's one rotten story in an
anthology, don't spend the entire review moaning
about it. If a book is almost entirely rubbish, don't
spend the entire review talking about the one thing
you liked and skating over the rest.

Among all the comments about Priest's review, I
didn't see a single suggestion that he didn't believe
what he said. They just thought he shouldn't have said
what he thought. That's not a view that is ever going to
gain ground with the kind of reviewer who prides
themself on their honesty.

Reviewers don't particularly expect anyone to enjoy
being reviewed, but authors don't set the rules for
reviewers, except in so far as they can ask their
publishers not to send us books – in which case,
whatever, we'll read something else. Trying to dictate
the terms of engagement is a waste of their time. We
don't take our cues from them, we don't write for
them.

It's like a potato trying to tell you which ketchup is

best. The ketchup isn't for the potato's benefit – it's for the consumer.

There's a tendency among some writers to regard reviewers as a service group, as an extension of their PR department, and unfortunately there are some bloggers who feel the same way, which confuses the issue. This kind of attitude to reviews – the idea that they should be "helpful" to authors and publishers, rather than to readers, or even worse, that they should be "constructive", as if reviewers are beta readers – is a bit too common among small press and indie authors and publishers (one reason we don't review them as often as we used to) and it's a shame to see it spreading to the mainstream. Perhaps that's down to the supposedly parlous state of publishing, more pressure coming to bear on those who might be seen as *traitors* to the cause of reading. Or maybe it's harder to hide a thin skin on social media, so authors are making it the job of others to protect their thin skins.

Reviews aren't exempt from criticism. As with the work of other writers, people will read our work and say what they think about it. But it's up to us how we go about it. When I write a novel, I don't worry for a minute what reviewers might think of it. I write the novels I want to write. If at some point a reviewer takes a liking to them, great, but I don't need that external validation to be happy with my work. A bad review still means someone read my book, and that's enough to make me happy in itself.

In my recent experience, a good deal of fantasy and science fiction books professionally published in the UK are three-star books. No gigantic flaws that render them unreadable, perfectly good entertainments, but not anything that'll be jostling for space in the pantheon. And generally I'm okay with that, and so is publishing – what matters to most publishers is what sells, what matters to most readers is what entertains.

But when the best writers come down from their eyries to remind us that flying higher is possible, let's thank them for it, rather than pretending they have a duty to protect our feelings.

Contributors

Antonella Coriander has (in this reality, at least) only ever been published in *Theaker's Quarterly Fiction*, to her great dismay. Her story in this issue is the second part of her ongoing Oulippean serial.

John Greenwood's stories have appeared in *Bourbon Penn* and *Rustblind and Silverbright*, but his most recent fiction for our own magazine seems to have been all the way back in 2010, when the long-running (and much-missed) saga of Newton Braddell came to a conclusion in #32. He returns to the front of house in this issue with "The Collection Agent".

Charles Wilkinson's publications include *The Snowman and Other Poems* (Iron Press, 1978) and *The Pain Tree and Other Stories* (London Magazine Editions, 2000). His stories have appeared in *Best Short Stories 1990*, *Best English Short Stories 2*, *Midwinter Mysteries*, *Unthology*, *London Magazine*, *Able Muse Review* and in genre magazines/anthologies such as *Supernatural Tales*, *Horror Without Victims*, *The Sea in Birmingham*, *Sacrum Regnum*, *Rustblind and Silverbright* and *Shadows & Tall Trees*. *Ag & Au*, a pamphlet of his poems, has come out from Flarestack and new short stories are forthcoming in *Ninth Letter* and *Bourbon Penn*. His story in this issue is "A Thousand Eyes See All I Do", which may somewhat surprise readers after the quiet horror of the previous stories we have published by him.

Douglas J. Ogurek's work has appeared in the *BFS Journal*, *The Literary Review*, *Morpheus Tales*, *Gone Lawn*, and several anthologies. He lives in a Chicago suburb with the woman whose husband he is and their five pets. In this issue he reviews the film *Maleficent*. His website: www.douglasjogurek.weebly.com.

Howard Watts is a writer, artist and composer living in Seaford who provides the cover art for this issue and a story too, "Contractual Obligations".

Jacob Edwards belongs in truth to Australia's speculative fiction flagship *Andromeda Spaceways Inflight Magazine*, but we're happy that he dabbles with us. This writer, poet and recovering lexiphanicist's website is at: www.jacobedwards.id.au. In this issue he reviews *Edge of Tomorrow*, *Ernest et Célestine*, *Star Wars: Maul – Lockdown* and *The Tripods*.

Stephen Theaker reviews too many things to list in this issue, but given that he has another twenty unfinished reviews on the go perhaps he should consider making them a bit shorter, hm? Or not trying to review absolutely everything he reads, hm? No one is interested in what he thinks about *Sabrina the Teenage Witch: 50 Magical Stories*! Anyway, his work has also appeared in *Black Static*, *Interzone*, *Prism* and the *BFS Journal*. His hobbies include the creation of new authorial pseudonyms and watching the arguments in Kickstarter comment threads.

Tim Atkinson makes his TQF debut in this issue with a review of *Apocalypse Now Now*. Tim lives, reads and works in the West Midlands. Sporadically he jots down thoughts about SFF and more at www.magpie-moth.blogspot.co.uk

Tim Jeffreys is another Tim making his first TQF appearance in this issue, with the story "The Riches".

He is a UK-based writer of horror and speculative fiction, whose work has appeared in various anthologies and magazines.

A Thousand Eyes
See All I Do

Charles Wilkinson

Queen Elizabeth scratched her balls. She was sitting
on the patio that overlooked the back yard and its
death of a lawn – clumps of sere grass, patches of
baked soil like dried blood; in the borders, not a hint
of efflorescence, just brittle stems – the texture of
cheese stalks at a cocktail party. And at the far end,
what had once been a series of water features:
ornamental ponds, the exposed concrete now a
curious mixture of cream and milk purple, the shade
of the half-healed pits in the skin left by acne. Eight
years after the permanent hosepipe ban, there was no
trace of the knot garden that Dudley had created in
her honour. The whole oblong space was enclosed by a
pastry-white wooden fence scabbed with a few brown
whorls. An old petrol mower was rusting in the
dilapidated summer house. But it was quieter than
usual and there was a slight breeze to relieve the
intense heat of an afternoon in July. Six unopened cans
of lager cooled in the ice bucket, where the Groom of
the Stool had placed them two hours before. Her new
pain killers had induced an unfamiliar sensation, a
dreamy numbness that she was anxious to prolong and
which she knew would not be compatible with
alcohol. For once, it was enough simply to stretch out a
hand, and rake her fingers through the water until she

found a small smooth ice cube that she would then permit to dissolve on her tongue.

Bobby Dudley came out through the French window. She half hoped that just before he stepped round in front of her he would have peered down her expensive white cleavage, bare at the top of her white cotton blouse. The top button of her red PVC shorts was undone and she knew that the line of her snaking cock was just visible. But she understood from the way that his eyes were turned inwards that he had been surfing again; the petulant lips – the look of someone who has just had fifteen results removed from his pages by Google. He said that he was only doing it to lose weight; that there was something about his dark illicit searches that deprived him of his appetite far more effectively than any slimming tablets. But she thought he was already quite slim enough. He must have lost at least a stone during the business with Andy Robsart.

"Francis said that it's something you'll really need to look into. We've simply no idea what he's doing on the estate?"

"The Dark Lady?"

"Yes."

"Just another little Emo techie freak. Don't worry about it."

"You know I really don't think he's singing directly to his listeners."

Queen Elizabeth lay back in the royal recliner so that all she could see was a broad blue sky finished to a high glaze. And, now that flying was definitively out of fashion, not a contrail to be seen. There was something frightening about all that flat perfection. Not even a dusting of powdery sugar-cloud to suggest that the hydrologic cycle was still, meteorologically speaking, a going concern.

"Your Majesty?"

"And so you're saying that I have to see Walsingham?"

"I think it might be advisable, Your Majesty."

Walsingham. No doubt a thoroughly capable old beard, but someone who seemed to have little sense of her as woman. Still that hardly mattered in the circumstances. He was not the most alluring physical specimen in the court. There were even rumours that he might be heterosexual, although thank heavens he had always had the wit to keep that to himself.

"And is he here?"

"No, not at the moment. Francis said he'd come by later. Provided that's convenient, of course."

She lifted a can of Carling Extra half way out of the water. It was still just cool enough to be worth drinking, but after a moment she allowed it to slip back unopened into the bucket with the faintest of plops. It had been pleasant in the garden. For once she just been able to sit quite vacantly by herself, without giving a thought to the marriage question or the problems that Devereux's dealers were having with Irish smack-heads and wino recusants down in that wilderness of Highgate's high rises, always the most indefatigably traitorous part of her realm. And there had been some very worrying developments recently – quite apart from O'Neil and his outfit having the temerity to set up their own little nest of crack dens and porn shops along with a nice little sideline running illegal rosaries and selling consecrated rave wafers cut with Epsom salts and sawdust. No, what had really worried her was that Walsingham's geeks had been quite incapable of finding out who had hacked into her email account and sent all the favourites on her contact list a link to an advert recommending a well-known proprietary brand of haemorrhoid ointment. She had needed to muster more than usual reserves of sang-froid and mental agility to deal with the ensuing crisis. Her allies, of course, were soon placated, but King Philip of Sutton Coldfield had sent an emissary on a Harley Davidson to hand in an official complaint. As Cecil had pointed out, it simply wasn't good diplomacy to suggest that one's political opponents, however much one might secretly dislike them, were suffering from severe rectal bleeding. Perhaps now, while she was still sober, could be the time to see Walsingham – and Cecil as well. She thought of that unappetising old grandee with his ancient cracked leather jacket, talk of cash flows and trade deficits, faded tattoos and nose ring. No doubt they would both bore her spunkless with lectures on borrowing requirements, the delicate balance of the inner and outer city relations and the lessons to be learnt from the insurrection in Acocks Green – and all before ending up with the ludicrous proposal that she should allow herself to be fucked up the arse by some mad bear from Walsall. But it had to be admitted that, whether she liked it not, they were probably the only two people in her entire entourage with more than a sliver of intelligence and integrity.

"How is the Royal Chest?" she asked.

"Ample, I should say," he said, looking down at her with respect. Half an hour ago she would have been pleased by this 1960s style comic sally, the interest in his eyes, the lascivious twist of his lips clearly visible in spite of his beard. But just thinking about Walsingham had acted as a powerful anti-aphrodisiac.

"You know perfectly well that I was wondering whether Cecil wants to talk about money."

"Oh, William always wants to talk about money," he said, flicking his fringe out his left eye.

She had once loved him so much, it was hard to believe. But had he ever loved her? They said that he murdered his boyfriend, poor pale Andy Robsart found with his delicate white neck broken at the

bottom of a flight of stairs. And still wearing a silly
little leather cap with a peak and a ring of studs,
though there were two injuries to his head, one the
depth of half a thumb, the other deeper. A very stupid
and clumsy way to dispose of someone, if that was
what he had done. But why – if he had committed this
act so that he could at last move into her bedchamber
– had he now taken up with the absurd Knollys twink?

"Text them both. Tell them I'll see them at six."

"What William as well? I think Francis might prefer
it if..."

"You heard, so just do it. And tell Walsingham that
if he's been pulling out anyone's fingernails he's to
wash his hands before he appears in my presence."

She stood up surprisingly swiftly and motioned for
Dudley to leave. As she watched his bum swaying
towards the French window, she felt a sudden deep
ache of desire. He would never hold her, regnant and
silver in her nakedness – she knew that now. The way
that he shut the door was just a little too loud to be
entirely consistent with protocol. The last bit of the
happiness that she'd taken from the day evaporated.

And everything in the garden – the dead
lawnmower, the dried-up grass, the flower beds' baked
clay, the tepid water in the ice bucket, the recliner
stained with sweat and sun lotion; and everything in
the garden – the raw concrete of the empty pond; the
shrivelled stick of a plant; the rotting wood of the
summer house; the irregular waves of grubby gravel on
the path; the abandoned water can; the discarded hose
pipe sloughed off like the skin of the snake; the shape
of vanished hedges hiding in the sub-soil; the brown
knot twisted into the untreated wood of the baby-
white fence – and everything in the garden seen
through the shimmer of the heat produced by the
repetition of the sinister blue and unendingly perfect
skies.

***

Walsingham's spy sat in the back seat of a saloon whose paintwork had been partially torched by a gang of youths two weeks previously. He had a good view of the house that he had been detailed to watch. It overlooked the entrance to the cul-de-sac in which Queen Elizabeth's palace, three former council houses knocked into one, was the solitary building of architectural interest. The property that he had under surveillance was the only one that was not owned by the Crown Estate. For over a quarter of a century it was home to two grey-haired bears, both remarkable for their personal sanctity and the probity with which they conducted the weekly S&M parties that had made them so affectionately regarded throughout the neighbourhood. Their soirées took place in a well-appointed dungeon, a hallowed space with walls of black leather and a fine collection of traditional instruments of torture. In the early days of her reign, Elizabeth had been so incensed by the bears' refusal to surrender the freehold of their property that Hawkins and Frobisher had been dispatched to quell their mutinous behaviour by employing certain well-tried nautical methods of persuasion. Unfortunately the bears had accepted their punishment with unalloyed relish. But in the end a modus vivendi was reached: in lieu of protection money, selected courtiers were given a tribute of five free tickets a month to the events of their choice. Even Cecil had been known to attend, sipping chilled Chablis on warm white wine evenings, stroking the handcrafted whips and exquisitely wrought wrist cuffs with his long and delicate fingers.

The spy ripped the cellophane off a white packet and shook out a cigarette. He smiled as he remembered the young man from the Oral B Jones Christian Community Centre whom he'd taken home the previous night. Although his catch had seemed diffident at first, it hadn't taken long for them to move from the aridities of disinterested theological enquiry to an intense exploration of each other's bodies. It was late when they finally shuddered to a halt and lay gasping in the bed, the moonlight mapping the silver contours of their bodies. In the morning, the man turned to a remorseful youth, talking of God as he helped the spy to change the stained sheets.

"There is no God," the spy had replied. "Only two screenwriters, a continuity editor and someone with a camcorder working in a converted warehouse in Digbeth."

And later, on the doorstep: "Kit, will I see you again?"

"Of course. If that's what you want. But you have to remember that there are some things that are far darker than sex."

The smoke was making him cough. Kit wondered whether the back right hand door of the saloon would drop off he tried to open it. A line of rusting and abandoned petrol cars stretched in front of and behind him. Hardly any had tyres and the glass in their windows had been smashed. Since the collapse in metal prices they weren't even worth towing off as scrap. A few of the bonnets were still up, a sign that someone had once thought them worth scavenging for parts. Of course all the radios and CD players had long since gone. When staking out a territory, it was important for one's vehicle to appear as inconspicuous as possible, and Dudley, as Master of the Queen's Motors, was always sure to ask the local lads to amuse themselves for an hour or two by distressing the bodywork and adding a spaghetti swirl of tags that were appropriate to the area. Kit's phone rang.

"The Dark Lady?" Walsingham's interrogative rasp.

"No sign of him."

"Well, stay there. I know that Gloriana wants this one sorted even though she won't admit it."

Three weeks after the death of the last bear in circumstances of an exotic and highly personal nature the house had been bought at an inflated price. Queen Elizabeth had still been in negotiations with the agents and had not been pleased to find herself gazumped, thus missing an opportunity to secure the western border of her realm. For a week there were no signs of activity in the house. Then painters and decorators arrived and a collection of racks, an assortment of restraining devices, including a magnificent throne of a chair with chains attached, a wardrobe of latex suits and a several leather collars with steel spikes were carried out and deposited near the withered rose bushes in the front garden. A day later an unmarked white van arrived with a large consignment of cardboard boxes and a platoon of technicians, enough geeks to install whole banks of computers. The venerable instruments of pain and delight were relegated to the skip, and the bears' garden, which since the great heat wave had admittedly been little more than a rubble of dry earth with a few etiolated plants haunting the shade under a dead brown tree, was tarmacked and divided into parking bays.

All attempts by Cecil's ambassador to open diplomatic relations with the new owner failed. It had been impossible to find contact numbers or an email address and no one ever answered the door; however, a bibulous office boy employed by the estate agents had, towards the end of an evening in the Black Horse, let slip that the buyer was Lucifrix Le Hayle. They were also given a description of a man who had been glimpsed leaving and entering by some of the local teenagers that Walsingham had asked to watch the place. Photographs showed someone of preternaturally youthful appearance who was always dressed in a well-cut black suit. His skin was strangely white and smooth, as if it was made of no ordinary substance but of silk or an unknown fabric of the flesh that would neither age nor tan. Le Hayle moved quickly, a shadow-flicker that passed from the front door to the driving seat of his petrol car in an instant. His times of arrival and departure were irregular, and on the few occasions that anyone had got close enough to shout out a question he neither answered nor turned in the direction of the speaker.

Kit was one of the team that Walsingham had assigned to watch the house in shifts. So far the target had made only short trips to the convenience store, none of which would have used up much fuel – although the fact that Le Hayle could run a petrol car at all suggested membership of the solvent elite, someone who could not only afford the high prices at the government garages but also had the influence to ensure continuity of supply.

It was just after eleven o'clock when Le Hayle came out the house, his right hand dipping into his pocket with gunslinger slickness before raising the barrel of his remote towards the car. Kit was too far away to hear the fat bullet *thunk* of the vehicle unlocking and then Le Hayle was behind the wheel so quickly that Kit couldn't even visualise him having had to open the door. In another second he was purring off down the road. Kit took out his phone and texted Walsingham. With so few vehicles on the road, it was all too easy to be conspicuous. It wouldn't take Walsingham long to rustle up a score of eyes to watch the route that Le Hayle was travelling and then their reports could be radioed back. Once he finished his cigarette, Kit turned the key in the ignition and the hybrid saloon slid effortlessly out onto the road. The machine felt good. Dudley, for all his foibles, could always be relied

upon to make sure that his motors were in excellent
order and well charged. It wasn't long before the first
sightings of Le Hayle. He was heading towards
Northfield in the direction of the Black Horse. Two
jeeps full of crossbow and beer can-toting Baggies fans
passed Kit and he moved gratefully into their
slipstream. They were going quite fast and so he put
his foot on the accelerator. It wouldn't do any harm to
close the gap a little. If Le Hayle decided to park the
car and continue on foot, his movements could be
harder for the informers to spot. A minute later
Walsingham himself was on the line saying that Le
Hayle had parked his car and was about to enter
Victoria Park.

Kit put the hybrid in the drive of a house that had
been burnt out during the most recent waves of riots.
That way Le Hayle would be less likely to notice it on
his way out. The sun climbed a blue-glass sky; the heat
bounced from the earth to the heavens and then back
again. Every speck of moisture had been wiped from
the air. A haze shimmered above tarmac that was
almost on the point of meltdown. As Kit crossed the
road, the soles of his shoes resisted his forward
movement, like plasters being peeled from the skin.
He went through the metal grey gate into the park.
This was the one place in Northfield that was exempt
from the hosepipe ban, a municipally green space,
with mature trees clad in unfamiliar bright foliage and
borders filled with shrubs, evergreens and some plants
that Kit could not name, their leaves the texture of
velvet, a soft silvery grey. Already the air was cooler.
There were litter bins of a type that had long since
been removed from most parts of the city. No doubt
the Trans-Mercian Government had decided that if
someone really wanted to blow up a park bench they
should be allowed to do so. If Le Hayle wanted to
make a drop, this was the ideal place for it. Kit looked

around. The lawns had just been mown and the smell
of cut grass lingered in the air. There was a hard tennis
court on which quite understandably nobody was
brave enough to play, and a children's play area with
custard-coloured slides and swings. Kit saw Le Hayle
walking up the path towards the basketball arena, a
sort of mini-stadium enclosed by a purple and orange
railing. To one side was a curious structure of late
modernist design, which had been painted in the same
clashing colours. It seemed that Le Hayle was just
about to make his way towards this spot when a wave
of excited teenagers, oblivious to the heat of the day
and about twenty strong, most in brightly coloured T-
shirts and cargo trousers, rushed along the path. Le
Hayle changed course and walked steadily towards
them, as if he were a swimmer who would show no
fear in front of the highest breaker. An outrider on a
skateboard swerved to avoid him, and then Le Hayle
seemed to vanish in an instant, as if he had
disappeared under their bobbing white headgear,
caught up in the crests and swirl of their movement.
Kit stood quite still, waiting for Le Hayle's head to
emerge, buoyed up on the currents of their joy,
perhaps with his mouth open, gasping for air, and
then a glimpse of his arms and hands stretching out,
changing shape like seaweed caught in the pull of the
tide, before he calmly resumed his progress up the
path. But there was no trace of him. Perhaps he had
reversed his direction and was now dancing and
roaring, jumping along them.

Kit watched the youths as they hurtled past but
there was no one wearing a dark suit, no one who
could possibly have been Le Hayle. Then Kit saw a
figure, almost at the perimeter of the park. It was hard
to be entirely sure that it was Le Hayle, but there was
something about the way he was moving – a pace that
seemed too quick to be accounted for by the act of

walking, although that was all the man appeared to be doing. Kit set off in pursuit and he was soon able assure himself that it was definitely Le Hayle, his face paler than ever, one black flap of hair covering half of his forehead and hanging down over his right eye. He was showing some interest in a building of red brick set in a well-kept little rock garden filled with miniature spruce and small shrubs that required little maintenance. The windows were covered by dark green corrugated shutters on to which a few arcs and curls of white graffiti had been sprayed like foam about to dissolve in sea-water. Le Hayle walked round the back of the building. It was hard to say what it had once been used for, but it stood next to what looked like an electricity sub-station – although this had a flagpole and was flying the cross of St George, a symbol of a nation that had been erased since the emergence of a new Heptarchy. Kit waited for five minutes and then made his way cautiously into the garden. Once again, Le Hayle was nowhere to be seen. A window had been bricked up and there was no door that could possibly have been opened.

As soon as Le Hayle came back out into the path, Kit saw him, walking swiftly in the direction of the wastepaper bin. He had one hand clasped to his chest, as if he were holding something, a large envelope perhaps, under his jacket. Then Kit realised with a sharp shock that Le Hayle was also standing by the children's play area, gazing at the empty swings and slides. Kit turned a full circle, scanning the park, and discovered three more figures who could all only have been Le Hayle: one was heading towards an exit from the park that lead to Northfield's main shopping area; a second was to be seen loitering between two cones, substitute goal posts left over from some game whose players had long since forsaken it; the third was making his way along an avenue of trees, the foliage a deeper and more innocent green than seemed possible in this time of blood and insurrection, as if every leaf had been borrowed from a legendary summer's day. Kit thought of one of Will's plays: "*I think there be six Richmonds in the field...*"

To have followed one Le Hayle would have been to lose the others. Kit contented himself with checking the litter bin – there was nothing in it apart from an empty beer bottle and couple of takeaway cartons that had probably come from a Chinese restaurant. He phoned Walsingham, tried to explain what had happened and arranged to meet at an inn nearby. As he turned off the main road, the scene of the ancient church and the public house nestling in a nook of what still looked almost like a quiet country lane, reminded him of the small village Northfield had once been, its only industry a few cottage workshops in which nails were made. As he got out of the car, he saw that cannon fire from the Emir of Bradford's mujahideen had destroyed a section of St Laurence's tower, slicing away the stonework like shale, leaving a sharp edge and the left side of the clock. The big hand was fixed at a fifteen minutes to an hour that had been blown away during the final artillery barrage. Since the Trans-Mercian Government had achieved a truce with the Southern Yorkshire Caliphate there had been several requests for compensation, but none had been forthcoming.

Cecil was sitting in the public bar of The Stone, two rooms that must have been knocked into one, the lineaments of an earlier age still evident in the low beams and uneven floor levels. Tobacco-stain light from yellow lamps mixed with the flare of plasma TV screens; middle-aged men, badly dressed in jeans, scuffed trainers and T shirts; garish menus with almost life-sized photographs of full English breakfasts and chicken tikka masala – everything ordinary and yet not quite so. There was something much older behind the walls, a conspiracy of immemorial spiders, delicate as the cracks in the paintwork – and waiting for nightfall: the suzerainty of silence and dust. Cecil was seated by himself at a table in the corner, a glass of sparkling rose untouched but within reach of his gloved right hand.

"Ah Marlowe," he said, with the irrepressible self-confidence of someone who had just built himself a bungalow in Barnt Green, "your last text made absolutely no sense whatsoever."

Christopher Marlowe shrugged and requested for himself a roughly cut near raw rump steak, a salad in a pool of watery blood, no chips, and a side order of onion rings. He tried to imagine Le Hayle naked, his elegant penis and tight scrotum – a lady's gun holstered in the finest white flesh. He lit a cigarette. *All those who love not tobacco and boys are fools.*

Queen Elizabeth struggled out of sleep to find that one of her dreams had been removed right from the very site of her innermost self. It was as if thieves had broken open the doors of the rich royal granary and carried out a glorious bale of hay, the one filled with the scent of ripe fields and the long blond days of summer. And now it was nearly morning and the vast barn of desire was almost empty: not one bird singing in the rafters, and nothing to put away to make bread in cold January. Only a few straws to be discovered by a puzzled ploughboy at the break of day.

When she had first awoken at four o'clock, she had told herself to write everything down and then store it away in a safe place, but she had been so anxious to submerge herself once more in a world of plenitude and colour that she had gone straight back to sleep. Now her dream was gone from her – although she knew that it was still out there somewhere: the words that she had whispered in a trance being argued over by semiologists; the small men with certificates in encryption skills paid to crack her symbols of sheaves and glinting sickles. Expose her majesty in a flash of light. *A thousand eyes see all I do.*

And now it was nine and they were all in her bedchamber: Cecil, Walsingham, Dudley, dear silly Hatton and even Essex man Devereux, just back from his failed mission in the bogs of Highgate, his slender neck almost ready to volunteer itself for the chop. Raleigh, with an offering of bling expropriated from armadas of yardies on their way to Aston, was shuffling towards her on his knees, the very picture of the archetypal sailor, artist and dwarf. It was too early to take it all in, but she had the impression that he was reciting a very bad poem – certain to be one of his own compositions – comparing her yet again to a moon made out of pure cocaine.

Then Cecil started up – his perennial theme: the desirability of her marrying some wealthy middle-aged bear with a big gaff in Solihull or Bromsgrove, instead of dissipating her energies in the pursuit of any passing piece of rough trade who imagined that he could sail up her Channel at will.

"Last time you wanted me to marry a midget from Kidderminster, but now you say it's not such a good idea."

"With respect, your Majesty, Philip of Lozells..."

"The one with the deformed spine?"

"A very minor physical abnormality, so slight, your Majesty, as to be barely noticeable..."

She stared at the ceiling. Don't agree to anything but rule nothing out. Oh what was the point of listening to them?

How many years gone since the Lord High Admiral with the key to her bedchamber? Early morning hide and seek, the angles of fresh day sunlight; the cold air tickles at dawn, the flat of his hand's soft-smart strokes, playful below the small of her back, loving the bounce of her. The twenty-six years between them. Her first lover taken at fourteen, though he never touched her there. Only the door of her chamber opening before she had dressed. His eyes wanting to see more. Although never all naked in front of him. And the outside sport: *romped in the garden and cut her gown in black cloth, into a hundred pieces.* Even now she sees his dead face in the small hours: the man with the drawn sword found in her brother's quarters. Her brother! Dear priggish early-to-be-dead Edward, saved for a few more years by a spaniel's bark.

"Your Majesty?"

"Yes."

Not Cecil thank God but Hatton. Lids, dear Lids.

"Yes, My Sheep."

"I have the plans here for your Summer Progress, your Majesty. You are the sun of this nation, the most glorious star in the sky, the light towards whom all must turn, both the most beautiful of sublunary beings and yet also the most perfect of all heavenly bodies..."

Now this was more like it. He knew how to flatter a girl and the gold-plated water closet that his friend Sir John had given her was one of the few presents that she not only liked but actually used.

And to proceed first to BetFred, which turf accountancy to be both aired and sweetened in anticipation of her arrival, and there a sum of moneys to be placed on the steed of her choice to run in the 2.15 at Uttoxeter. And from thence at a speed not exceeding miles five miles an hour to Mr Wu's Bamboo Garden, to accept the presentation of one chicken chow mein with special fried rice.

A great tenderness for all her subjects: the emo in the small bedroom self-harming to the sound of the voice singing of the emo self-harming in a bedroom decorated with stain-clouds and rain; the seven types of goth to be seen sitting in the mud and the bird shit in Pigeon Park; the greaser with the faded red and lilac tattoos blossoming on his forearms; the pornographer in the shop with the one naked light bulb, his bad skin the sheen of cellophane, or the sweat-slither on the palms of his customers' hands; the man with the widow's peak, the grey hair straight back over skull, the ponytail with the frayed ends – and his small bets with William Hill and Ladbrokes; the punters in the shop with the one naked light bulb who do not meet each other's eyes, taking the flesh of their lovers in orange boxed sets to the till; the old rocker with the novelty coffin and the line of dark followers; the man with seven nights of silence a week and one pint on the lonely table in the back bar; the tramp with the blue-steak face in Outpatients, two fingers angled across the gap where the cigarette used to burn; the early morning man outside the chemist waiting for the prescription that ends the night; the man bent over the sink, both taps on full, watching his blood mix with the water – the night of the razor moon. And the small bedroom with the walls that move in, harming the emo singing the stain-cloud rain song.

After they had all left – her advisers, her lovers, those who plumed themselves on being of the Government and Wardens of Her Manor, the Groom of the Stool entered at the precise speed permitted by the regulations drawn up by the Steward of the Household (see Section XXXIV para 3: On Approaching the Sovereign with an Anal Suppository). Flat on the palm of his extended right hand lay a silver salver on which rested a cloth of purple on which rested a triangle of grease proof material on which rested a pale and solitary gherkin of relief, aerodynamically perfect, infused with all the most efficacious opiates of the East, to be inserted at her Majesty's pleasure.

Queen Elizabeth walked over to the divan and lay there face down: soon the expert hands adjusting her undergarments; then the soothing unguents, followed by one swift forward thrust, the sphincter's grateful swallow before the pain fading from her ring of fire, her coronet of flames.

From inside a pocket of shade, Kit Marlowe looked out at a midday glare so intense that he suspected the sun was threatening to absorb all the colours of the street, returning them to whiteness. The overhanging branches under which he was crouched had cast a filigree of blue-black shadows around him. There was no wind so that by staying quite still it was possible to avoid the holes of light being burnt into the ground. He was under a tree just to the left of the back entrance to Northfield Station. He would see any passengers who came out before they had a chance to spot him.

Walsingham's spies had texted to say that Le Hayle had been seen boarding a train at New Street from which he had not yet alighted. Almost an hour had passed and Kit was just beginning to suspect that Le Hayle had vanished in transit when he saw him leaving the station. He was carrying a laptop so slim that it was as if it were in the instant of being forged like a blade: slender metal and white hot – ready to burn as it cuts. There was no car parked nearby and no one to meet him. It appeared that in spite of the intensity of the heat Le Hayle was prepared to travel on foot. Kit abandoned any idea of going back to the hybrid. At midday there were few cars on the road, and most of the populace would remain inside behind blinds or in the cool basements that had been dug deep into the earth. To drive now would only have attracted attention. They were in a woody area, undulating, with small suburban houses and winding roads. Le Hayle set off past the green railing and under the bridge. Whenever Le Hayle turned a corner, Kit would quicken his pace to ensure that there was no chance of his quarry slipping unseen down a side road. But it was just after Kit entered a wider road lined by large comfortable houses with spacious driveways and lawns at the front that Le Hayle disappeared. Kit stood still for moment. His shirt had stuck to his back and he could feel a serration of cold sweat marking a way down from his eyebrow to his chin. He looked around. There was not a car on the wide blank road or a cat or dog sunning itself on a lawn. It was then that he saw Le Hayle. He was no longer carrying his laptop, and, although his eyes were pointing straight ahead and he did not seem to be aware of Kit's presence, his right hand was inside his jacket, over the left side of his chest, as if he were ready to draw a knife straight from his heart.

Kit carried on up the street. He turned round and saw that Le Hayle had crossed the road, but did not appear to be trying to close the gap between them. Nevertheless, Kit decided to walk as quickly as was advisable in the heat; once, he almost broke into a run before stopping abruptly. It occurred to him that if he moved too fast he might come round a bend suddenly only to find the Le Hayle that he had been following earlier yards away from him on the pavement. This he told himself could not happen. Dr Dee had been most insistent that Le Hayle's apparent omnipresence in the park had been a kind of prestidigitation, a conjuring trick of a higher order that enabled Le Hayle to place disturbing illusions in the mind of his pursuers. No doubt he had simply slipped down a side road, doubled back and then used his undoubted turn of speed to appear from behind. When Kit next turned round, he could see no trace of his pursuer. He decided to walk to the hybrid. The handle of the car door was so hot that it almost burnt him when he touched it. Kit texted Walsingham, giving him the exact location that he had last seen Le Hayle and then drove towards the centre of Northfield. He decided to take an hour or so off. Perhaps if he stopped following Le Hayle this might yield better results. It was hard to deny that Le Hayle seemed to be so precisely aware of the intentions of his pursuers that he was able to deflect any threat to himself with such infuriating ease. It seemed preferable to go about one's business as normally as possible without giving a thought to Le Hayle. That way if one did happen to stumble across him it was just possible that he would be caught unguarded: his immaculate mental defence systems unable to track a malign intention that had not been consciously formulated in the more accessible areas of the mind.

In the back seat of the car was a document wallet that contained Kit's story about the Devil. He had decided, in defiance of advice from Walsingham and Cecil, that its merits should not go unnoticed by the world. But before sending it out to a publisher who had expressed an interest in seeing it he would have to take a copy. Since the postal workers had joined an occult sect devoted to the worship of a former manager of West Bromwich Albion, mail deliveries had been unreliable. Anything posted on a Saturday would be opened and all valuable contents removed and classed as offerings to the Black Country deity.

As he drove up towards the main shopping area, he saw the Black Horse, a vast galleon of an inn, black and white beams, mullioned windows, high gables, a stepped roofline with tiny bays, chimney stacks, a 1920s take on Tudor England, a brewer's vision of

Elizabethan glory, riding the crest of the hill: the red-bricked terraces that trickled down the hill, the Chinese restaurant, the hair dressers, the pawnbrokers, the discount stores – all tiny in its wake. He parked the hybrid, picked up the document wallet and made his way towards Knight's Pharmacy, Fax and Photocopying Services. Although there was little traffic, a caution bred into him since childhood – the cobbler's child has an eye that watches as the nail is struck into leather – he looked both ways. A lace curtain parted in the window above The Babylon Amusements. He tried not to glance up again. If he did, he knew that he would see versions of Le Hayle observing him from the mean windows above hairdressers, pet shops, money changers, estate agents and bargain basement shops. It was impossible, however, to be unaware that someone was watching him from under the orange awning of the Clock Café. He couldn't see whether it was Le Hayle.

The minute the door of the pharmacy closed behind him he realised that the place must have changed hands. What had been a cool clean space with glass-fronted cabinets filled with perfumes, all the stock neatly arranged in bright packaging, was a dim cave with yellow walls the colour of some thin liquid retched up from the stomach of a starving cat. Misshapen bottles of varying sizes, mostly made of blue and green glass, rested on shelves of warped wood. There was a counter, behind which sat a small woman with unnaturally black hair and a face of mahogany. Kit could just see through a hatch to the room that the pharmacist had occupied, but now there were no assistants in white coats holding pale green prescriptions slips: only a solitary physician in a pointed hood and a cloak, his face covered by a mask with a long beak that might have belonged to a giant bird.

Kit was about to leave when he saw a photocopier standing in the corner.

"May I use your photocopier?" he asked the woman.

"A poultice of onion, garlic and butter..."

"No, your photocopier. May I use it?"

She nodded and waddled off in the direction of the hatch. The machine was pea-coloured and of a make with which Marlowe was unfamiliar. He examined it. There were several symbols that he had not seen before. Nevertheless, he fed his papers in and pressed the green button. Within seconds, the machine was swiftly and smoothly sliding out copy on top of copy. Then it stopped. Pleased, Marlow picked up his manuscripts and was about to go back to the counter to pay when he heard the machine whirr once more before starting to deal out duplicates with card-sharp slickness. After a minute, it paused once more before beginning the third set.

Kit turned round but there was no one at the counter.

"How do I stop this thing?"

The paper was buckling and curling in the tray, and then spilling on to the floor. Kit picked up two sheets: one was a scene from near the beginning of his story; the second was in Arabic. Kit jabbed at several buttons, but nothing could interrupt the smooth running of the machine. He told himself that he must not panic. He looked at the control panel; there were no words, only symbols, not all of which he had noticed earlier, most no more than a few lines placed at odd angles or next to a dot. He was about to shout for help when he realised that the woman was standing beside him. She lifted the lid of the machine and drew back her sleeve to expose a white cauterised stump, which she slid gently over the platen as if she were wiping a mirror. The machine ejaculated one final sheet of paper and finished with a sigh.

"You must pay, pay for all these writings," she said.

"Yes, of course I'll pay. At least I'll pay for what is my work. Some of this isn't even in English."

"No, you pay for everything… all writings. I give you amount in minute."

"We'll see about that."

Kit sat down on a small, three-legged stool of the type that women used when milking cows and began to sort through the papers. Everything was jumbled up. Most of the work was undoubtedly his, although several scenes had been translated into bad French, and there was a whole chapter in which every other line was in Russian. The woman was back behind the counter now, working on a calculator. Kit stood up and put the papers down in front her.

"How much?"

She named a ridiculous price.

"I'm not paying that. Some of this is definitely not mine. I mean what about this?" He picked up a sheet covered in script filled with letters, shapes and signs arranged in a manner that bore no approximation to anything that he had ever come across.

She looked at it and then said "Is yours. Is your Devil story in future language. All writings is yours."

"Well, I'm not paying. Your machine's completely out of control."

"Is for you to check setting of machine."

"I'm not paying."

She picked up the manuscripts. "Then I keep these."

"You can't do that. They're my intellectual property. Where's the manager? Tell him I want to speak to him."

The physician had come to the hatch and was staring down his long beak into the room: a bird on some remote shore that Kit could never visit. There was a smell of vinegar and bergamot. Behind his mask, wrapped in the miasma of his smells, he was almost safe from the plague.

"I is all managers here. Either you pay or I keep."

Kit took out his wallet and slammed down a fistful of notes, approximately half of what he owed. As she picked up the money to count it, Kit grabbed his manuscript and fled. It was only a minute later that he realised that some deep part of mind, fed by his peripheral vision, had half noticed a dark figure, flickering out of the Clock Café just seconds after he had left the pharmacy. This image, which he had stored just below the level of consciousness, had now surfaced and was awaiting development.

Walsingham had arranged a meeting at the Black Horse. As Kit walked back down the hill towards the inn, he noted how the building looked so much smaller from that perspective, the half-timbering deliciously softened by its proximity to an annex of honeyed fudge in Cotswold stone. Inside, the odour of paint from a recent refurbishment mingled with the scent of charred steaks. The place had an air of opulence that was unfamiliar in this part of the city: leaded glass, great baronial stone fireplaces, one with a carving of the Black Horse, decorated ceilings in the style of the Arts and Crafts Movement, which was somewhat at odds with the shabby drinkers lined up at the long bar. Girls with piercings and too much make-up ate in dignified dining-areas with mullioned windows. Waitresses hurried past carrying plates heavy with all-day traditional breakfasts. A giant plasma TV screen showed a bald footballer scoring the same goal from five different angles. Again and again the ball hit the back of the net, the player skidded across the grass on his knees, his fist clenched, his upper body leaning back, the full lips wide and open, as if ready for an act of fellatio.

To attract the barmaid's attention, Marlowe drew

his sword halfway out and then slammed it back hard into its sheath. He could feel a damp ring of sweat underneath his ruff. As the girl hurried towards him, her plucked eyebrow raised in enquiry, Marlowe remembered that he was supposed to be meeting Walsingham upstairs. He registered her look of bewilderment at the very moment he began to move away from her.

He walked out of the bar, through a lobby, under an arch and then up a staircase with carved balustrades, impeccably polished. At the top there was a tiny landing. A sculpture of a black stag had been placed in a curious rectangle, which was made of wooden slats and roughly the height of a child's play pen. The stag, its antlers on a head that seemed too small to support the weight, faced the door. Kit turned the handle and entered. In front of him was a small room with a barrel-vaulted ceiling beautifully decorated with gilt strips, their motif of vine leaves and birds apparently frozen in the act of almost eating grapes. There was a wooden settle, the lustre of polished tables, and armchairs upholstered in ox-blood leather. There was no one behind the small bar and not a noise apart from a low electrical hum, possibly a fridge. Beyond was a banqueting hall with flying beams and another huge stone fireplace, this time with a relief of a man's nut-small head. It was quite impossible to hear anything from downstairs. The knives and the forks glimmered, waiting for some great event.

It was odd that there no sign of Walsingham, normally a punctual man. Kit flicked open his mobile. There were no messages. As he put it back into his pocket he realised that he was no longer holding the document wallet that contained his story about the Devil. There was nothing on any of the tables or chairs. He had either left it downstairs on the bar or it was on the back seat of the car. Then suddenly he felt the absolute certainty there was someone outside on the landing. He went back into the bar and opened the door. Only the stag, its eyes sealed and death-mask blank. Not a footfall on the staircase. As soon as he stepped back into the bar, he saw Le Hayle on the settle. He was wearing a black suit with a white shirt and a thin black tie. His left eye was hidden beneath an ebony waterfall of hair. A laptop lay on the table in front of him, its screen facing away from Kit.

"Drink?" said Le Hayle.

Kit nodded and as Le Hayle walked over to the bar he went round to the other side of the table and looked at the screen. It was open on the last page of his story about the Devil. For once, Le Hayle appeared to be in no hurry and Kit had resumed his place in the middle of the room by the time that a tall frosted glass was offered to him.

"You know," said Le Hayle quietly, "if one does visit the Pharmacy of Night it is always a good idea to settle one's account in full."

History repeats itself but with variations.

Le Hayle picked up his laptop and ripped off the keyboard revealing a space that was far deeper than anything that could have been imagined. Kit saw his story tremble, about to go out. And from the bowels of the machine came a knife that was not the knife that had killed Kit the last time, though its edge was just as sharp – could cut any finger of sunlight that it touched.

O for a doughnut of air, for Liz to sit on, she thought. They were all there in front of her, except for Frobisher who was still out chasing Walsall gold. It was three weeks since her operation, the big one, and none of them could come up with anything better than the inflatable pumpkin cushion on which she was positioned so painfully, the hideous orange material from which it was made clashing terribly with her hair. And nothing had quite prepared her for the pain. This morning she had stopped putting on her white face when she realised that it was less white than her own skin. What she had asked them to find was simple: a pink inflatable cushion with a hole in the middle like a doughnut. Something that would provide proper support for her posterior whilst ensuring that the royal anus and its contiguous territories remained suspended over nothing more abrasive than a void. It was hard to believe that they were concentrating. Cecil would speak of nothing save for the forthcoming treaty with Redditch, Walsingham was in a strop because one of his spies had been knifed to death in an upstairs room at the Black Horse, and Essex, fresh from his humiliations in Highgate, could only talk of war against Kidderminster, a diversionary tactic of course. Still at least she had pretty little Hatton to look at, a man so beautiful, so ethereal, that even his underpants had been spun out of the webs of money-spiders. And now here was someone, yet another beard, whom she could only just recognise, it could have been Effingham but she was not sure, banging on about poor parenting skills on the Longbridge estate. She thought of her own merry monarch of a father: burst belly like two mountains thrown up by the movement of tectonic plates, a great red rump steak of a face, suppurating ulcers on both legs, reeling back every night from the Stone, with an afterwards of two six packs of Stella Artois and three bottles of blond Belgian Leffe beer (5.1% proof) in a plastic bag. Then Ann Boleyn, raging again headless through the sleep hours, her blood shining on the block, every nightmare's worst mother.

"And, I regret to say, your Majesty, what has been recovered from the hard-drive provides clear proof of heterosexuality. Indisputable evidence of visits to such websites as..."

Walsingham again. Always indefatigable in his pursuit of the transgressive, the sexual heretic. Today he was dressed in a fine robe trimmed with fox fur, worn over a purple T-shirt emblazoned with a picture of the Communards, pointed shoes with silver buckles from God knows what century – and tight leather trousers, standard issue. And round his shoulders, a tippet, being of white wool, which did stream down to his knees, purled like a river that doth run over stone. A jumble of monitors, part of an Apple Mac, a beaten up laser printer and five laptops were parked on the table in front him. All discovered in some stinking priest hole in an old warehouse near Hurst Street.

"Take all that rubbish away," she snapped. *"I have no desire to make windows into men's souls."*

A sudden thrill of trumpets. The entry of the fool, her dwarfs, the blackamoor of the week, the shepherds and nymphs of Diana, tumblers and five retainers liveried in frilly white silk shirts open down to the navel, each boy bearing a tasselled rug worked in needlepoint upon which lay the recommended articles of posterior support, requested from eBay and sites vetted by the Privy Council and the Under-Master of the Jakes. On Approaching the Sovereign with an Inflatable Plastic Cushion. Section MXV paragraph II: An exact speed of not more than two miles an hour to be maintained, a manner at all times reverent and of the utmost sobriety...

"Not now, not now," she screamed. How to uphold her body's celestial integrity with these daily reminders of its imperfections? And in front of so many people too. "Can't you see that we've matters of state to discuss. Dudley, make yourself useful for once and just get rid of them."

He was seated to her right and she could see that he

was surfing the net on his mobile. The Lone Ranger was doing something vile to a naked Tonto whilst Silver looked on with commendable equine restraint. Dudley – well, he was the Earl of Leicester although you'd never think it – looked up at her with a pout.

"Now, Cousin, now," she snapped.

She watched him as he ran-walked in their direction, waving his arms and wriggling his bum huffily.

Afterwards an audience with Cecil. The files were still going missing: sometimes destroyed or degraded; occasionally hidden behind an icon, along with the dead saints, the records of dissolved chantries, the fragments of illuminated manuscripts rescued from the ruins and then forgotten. Someone had stolen all the old video-tapes – the scenes of gardens, fountains, and innocent walks down avenues of tall trees – and wiped them: Katherine Parr's home movies gone. Emails from those who loved her were being sent straight to junk. Walsingham feared an all out cyber attack. They had their defences: firewalls in all the Cinque ports and Hawkins sailing up and down the Marche in a dinky little *bateau* bristling with cannon. A new program that scanned for spyware, could smell a Jesuit at fifty paces, was on order. But there were days when it was hard to believe they weren't being had: half their data and even the back up shafted, the rest circulating freely in cyberspace, read by a thousand eyes on the web. And who was responsible? She had met him once. After long negotiations he had arrived at Nonsuch, dressed in black, his skin so pale, one of his eyes hidden beneath a slick of his hair. As he entered the door, he was sitting down in front of her, their eyes level. How did you do that? she'd asked. Then again he was the shape of a shadow slinking through the door at the very moment that the shape of a man or a shadow or a boy who was a shadow and a

man was sitting – yes, right there on the very spot
where they'd all bowed and sunk to their knees – in
front of her. On the authority of clock and of candle
and of sundial, it was known that they had spoken for
one hour. She remembered not a word that was said.

At least now, your Majesty, it is time for a Summer
Progress. Thank you, Cousin. Already she can hear the
music and the sound of rejoicing. The Master of the
Motors has souped up an old Austen 7 from the glory
days at Longbridge and sprayed it pink. Out on to the
Bristol Road. The cheering populace. Behind her the
jeeps, her musicians, the sound of hautboys, viols and
bass guitars; shawns, sackbuts and the twang of a
Fender Stratocaster; an open-topped white van and a
combo jazzing on spinet, dulcimer and cornet. Dead
Sir Philip Sidney on bass guitar, Fulke Greville on
synthesiser and Drake on drums. On up the
thoroughfare, past the Money Shop, loans on jewellery
– gold bought any condition; summer escapes to the
Corfu and the Canaries; hair, cut and finish; Uncle
Money T.V. you can always trust your uncle; hair, cut
and finish; cash converters, spread the cost, no credit
check – Cecil, why are the people so poor? I don't
know, Your Majesty; Cool Trader, best value in frozen
hearts; this Shopping Centre with over six hundred
spaces for cars to be catacombed; hair, cut and finish.

Although she does not turn round, she knows that
her train is coming up the hill behind her: three
hundred carts, the spare royal bed, her hip bath,
moving to the accompaniment of pipes, mouth-
organs, kazoos and tabors. Apartments at the Plough
and Harrow and the Green Man have been cleaned
and the air sweetened with herbs. But tonight she is
staying in her room at the Crown in Digbeth. Twice
the alarm has sounded for intruders but no one has
been discovered. It is midnight. Her walnut bed is
carved with the heads of the Royal Beasts; an arras is

stitched with Pelicans, who pluck their breasts to feed their young. The moonbeam is an ermine that would die rather than besmirch its chaste white coat. It is warm and she is naked, sprawled over a space made for two. She thinks, as she has done every night for years, of her one chance: Seymour in her bedchamber. He is up with the dew on the grass. She hid behind the curtain, then peeked out, smiled. Nothing happened, though they romped. Later, she told them, the old inquisitors, no one had touched her there. Now even Seymour was fading – his smile not remembered as it was; his eyes changing one shade of colour each night. How long before she would recall nothing?

And then the noise, the faint music of logging on. She sits up. The Dark Lady of desire and technology, the master of the trace and the sensuous moment, is seated beside her and smiling. "Don't worry," he says – his laptop rests between his thighs – "I have all your dreams, quite safe, in here."

Beatrice et Veronique: Into the Island

Antonella Coriander

It was true, Beatrice discovered. She was a robot. The cloth of her jacket and shirt was scorched and torn across her back, and her fingers touched metal. The metal that was her. She lifted and lowered her shoulders, and felt the metal shift under her fingers.

"This isn't possible," said Beatrice.

Veronique nodded. "I would have said the same."

"There's no way I am a robot. It simply can't be."

"And yet you are. Look on the bright side, Beatrice, at least you're a whole robot, rather than half a robot. Despite the circumstances, I'm envious of you right now."

Beatrice shook her head. "I've been wounded in the course of duty. I've been operated on. If I were a robot someone would have spotted it before now."

Veronique would have shrugged, had she recovered the use of her shoulders. "Either your true nature managed to conceal itself—"

"Hypnotism, you mean?"

"Something like that, yes. Or, even if you are a robot now, you were not a robot then."

"I became a robot at some point?" said Beatrice. "Without knowing. It seems far-fetched."

"And yet you are one. Remember, we were out cold before waking up here, and we still don't know where here is. Though we have an inkling that the egg of a crystal dinosaur is what brought us here."

"Good grief."

Looking down at Veronique on the sand, Beatrice realised how selfish she was being. Yes, she had a lot to take in, but that went double for Veronique.

"Let me help you up." She bent down and lifted Veronique, carrying her over to lean against a tree. That felt a bit more civilised.

Veronique's arms had begun to twitch a bit. "I think I'm starting to get the hang of this."

"We might not be who we think we are," said Beatrice. "We might just be copies of the originals. Replicas."

"But we could also be downloads," said Veronique. "We shouldn't assume that we're copies just because we're robots. We were hit by lightning, after all. Perhaps our bodies were destroyed and our minds saved. Maybe our new robot bodies were being flown from Japan and there was a crash and we survived it."

Beatrice shook her head. "A good theory, but we still had the Queen's Wonder with us, and we are wearing the same clothes – in my case, exactly the same clothes, even down to loose stitches in exactly the same places."

Veronique thought about it for a few moments before replying, staring out at the ocean, letting the waves calm her anxiety. "Whether we're copies or not," said Veronique, "I don't want to die. Whatever I am, I want to live, I want to keep going. Even if I'm a copy of the original me, now that I exist I want to live on. I want to know where we are, what's on this island, who did this to us. For all we know, the original Beatrice and Veronique are somewhere on this island, and could still be rescued."

Beatrice agreed, and decided that the first step was to search the beach for any signs of their bicycles. As robots she guessed they wouldn't have much use for medical supplies any more, but she needed materials to make a stretcher for what was left of Veronique. But there was no sign, even after walking thirty minutes along the coast in each direction.

Returning to Veronique, she explained that the mission had been unsuccessful.

"Never mind, thanks for trying," replied Veronique. "Just get some branches from a tree. Apparently I'm a robot now, so comfort isn't a priority."

"I wonder if we need any food," mused Beatrice. "I don't feel hungry, even after my walk."

"I don't even feel pain now," said Veronique. "It's as if a spell has been broken. I'm still aware of the damage, but it's like a report now, not a feeling."

Beatrice took off her jacket and ran two branches through its sleeves. She tied the jacket to the branches at its four corners. It didn't seem strong, given all the rips and tears, but it was made of tough material, and she hoped it would support Veronique in her diminished state. With luck it wouldn't have to cope with the fire-breathing attacks of any more crystal dinosaurs. That was a one-off, she decided with deliberately blind confidence.

"All aboard!" shouted Beatrice, with a forced jolliness for which she immediately apologised. She lifted Veronique onto the stretcher and then considered which way to go. She had seen nothing on her walk which encouraged further exploration in either direction.

Then she noticed something rather odd about the crystal dinosaur. It was beginning to crack and crumble, so quickly it was almost completely gone by the time she had swung the stretcher around for Veronique to see.

"Good riddance!" said Veronique. "No one bites off the lower half of my body without coming to regret it!"

"Look!" said Beatrice, pointing to where the crystal dinosaur had hit the treeline. "There's a way off the beach!"

The falling dinosaur had flattened enough of the trees that Beatrice could actually see beyond them to blue skies. She had no idea what the island's interior might hold, but it was better than staying here on the beach. The seaside was no place for a robot. She didn't want to rust.

She dragged the stretcher towards the gap. As she passed between the trees she had the oddest sensation that she was being watched by a thousand tiny eyes. Perhaps she was; perhaps she had new senses in this robot body. But it hardly took special senses to guess that this dense greenery would provide a home to a myriad of tiny creatures. She hoped none of them were deadly (though what could hurt her now?) and kept walking.

If she had been hoping to get a good view of the island from here, she was disappointed. She could see up to the sky, but the views directly ahead and to left and right were blocked by hills. They were too small to deserve the name mountains, but they were rocky and climbing them would not be easy, especially with Veronique in tow. She decided to head south, and try to skirt the lowest of them. If getting around it proved impossible, that would probably be the least difficult to climb.

So off she trudged, dragging an uncomplaining Veronique behind. The ground was rough, rocks and pebbles doing their best to twist her ankles while vines and bushes tried to hook her feet. But she kept going, since there was nothing else to be done.

"It's weird," said Veronique, "how the treeline is so regular. It makes sense from the other side, since the trees can't grow very well in sand, but why does it stop so suddenly on this side?"

Beatrice hadn't really noticed, but turning to look north like Veronique she saw it very clearly. She couldn't see the beach from here, but the line of trees seemed to parallel exactly the line of the coast. She couldn't see any spots where the trees spread into the interior.

She turned back and carried on walking. "Perhaps there's a narrow band of fresh water, or good soil."

"Could be," said Veronique. "But I wonder if someone planted them like this."

"I haven't seen any footprints, and I'd swear we were the first to walk this way."

"Someone who cared about their privacy might like it this way. Imagine that we are still back in the English Channel. We could have blundered into a place, step by step, that someone has worked very hard to keep quiet."

Beatrice nodded, then felt like an idiot, realising Veronique could not see her. "A hidden island, ringed by trees, and the Queen's Wonder – it could have been taken from here originally."

"A guard dog, ready to chase intruders around the outside of the fence."

"But someone got it off the island, took it to London, and then you brought it back."

"My bad," said Veronique.

"Your bad indeed," said Beatrice. "It doesn't look like I will be taking you back to England for trial, but I think you've had your comeuppance."

"Lesson well and truly learned, your honour. I will never steal again."

They had been walking for, Beatrice would have guessed, a couple of hours before night began to fall. What a day, she thought to herself. Or at least she thought it was herself. Whatever. Until she knew otherwise she was going to act like Beatrice Gill. She would hold herself to Beatrice Gill's ethical standards. She would assume she was Beatrice Gill. She would sing when Beatrice Gill would have felt like singing and she was going to cry when Beatrice Gill would have felt like crying.

Other options were available, but that was the choice she made. She thought it was the choice Beatrice Gill would have too.

And right now, she thought Beatrice Gill would have chosen to make camp for the night. Even robots could fall down chasms in the dark. It might even be worse for her than a human. If she became trapped in a pit, she might be there for years, going slowly (or perhaps quickly!) insane, before her power unit eventually gave out.

From the moment the light had begun to fade she had been keeping an eye open for a suitable spot. Without a tent or other camping gear, of course, nowhere was *very* suitable. But eventually she found a place where a rock jutted out just far enough to provide them with a bit of shelter should it rain. She got Veronique into a comfortable position first, then leaned the stretcher against the rock to provide her with a little extra cover.

Beatrice settled down to rest. Without her jacket, she knew that she should begin to feel cold, and when she concentrated on it she became aware of internal communications telling her that she was. She would have to be careful about that. Being spared the pain of the day's battles was a mercy, but what if she didn't notice something important? She still had ninety per cent of her skin and she wanted to keep it that way as long as possible. Maybe she wasn't human any more – if she ever had been – but she wanted to play at being one as long as she could.

The women agreed to take turns on watch. Both felt the need to sleep; presumably it performed for their robot bodies a similar service to that it performed for humans. Perhaps it wasn't just the brain that needed sleep, but the mind, in so far as the two things may logically be divided.

Beatrice took the first watch, and was pleased to see Veronique drop off to sleep very quickly. It had been an *extremely* tiring day. Her watch was uneventful. There was a full moon, and visibility was about as good as it could have been. One worry was that she couldn't see very far, due to the ups and downs of the terrain. If any wild animals attacked she might have just a few moments to respond.

If only she knew where they were: that would have helped her to prepare for any dangers. On an island of this size off the coast of Scotland she'd be looking out for wolves. Near Florida she'd be looking out for alligators. India and her worry would be tigers. Canada, it would be bears. If they were still in the England Channel, there wouldn't naturally be any dangerous predators here, except maybe a snake or two. But there was nothing natural about this place.

Soon it was her turn to sleep, and Veronique kept watch. Beatrice curled around her, partly for warmth, partly so that they would both be hidden behind the stretcher, and partly so that Veronique would be able to wake her quickly by voice alone. Veronique had as yet managed nothing more than a few distinct shivers with her arms, and that would be no good if a snake attacked.

Beatrice dreamed of home, of visiting Mum's house on a Sunday. Olu ghobi at half past eleven, exactly. Having a cup of hot sweet tea, made in a pan. A kettle was good for an everyday cup of tea, but Sundays it had to be done in the pan, with a mysterious masala of spices that Beatrice had never been able to get quite right herself. In the dream her mum was stroking her head, just like when she was poorly. Beatrice could always tell when her Mum was worried about her, because she let her watch science fiction programmes without complaint. More usually, they would watch cosy detective programmes together. *Mrs Columbo*, *Murder She Wrote*, *The Librarian Says Shush*, *Mrs Gill Investigates*. That last one always made them laugh. On the television this time was *Space University Trent*, so Beatrice knew she must be poorly. She'd never seen this episode before. The faculty staff were all blind— no, worse than that, their eyeballs were dangling from their sockets, wobbling back and forth as they tried to investigate what was happening. Beatrice asked her mum to turn it over. It was making her feel ill. Mum didn't respond, so Beatrice turned to look at her. Mum's eyeballs were hanging out of their sockets too.

She wanted to wake up screaming, but she needed the sleep and toughed it out. Who knew? It might be the last time she got to see her mum.

Eventually she was woken up by Veronique, who was gently whispering at her. "Time to wake up, Beatrice."

"How was it?" asked Beatrice.

"Quiet, luckily. I can hardly keep my eyes open. But I can do this." She was able to move her arms just enough to shift herself into a reclining position. "Good night."

"Good night," said Beatrice. "Sleep well. Hope your dreams are better than mine."

Beatrice settled herself in for the watch. She realised, not without some pleasure, that she now felt rather thirsty. They hadn't given it any thought since the discovery that they were both robots. But apparently whatever kind of robots they were, they were the kind that needed to drink. There was nothing she could do about it now. One more watch, then she could sleep again, and then they could make finding water their priority. She should think about getting food, too. She hadn't expected to need that either, but if a need for water was affecting her now, a need for food would surely follow. Her guess was that whoever had built them had built in this need to help them emulate their human counterparts all the better. The need built in, she would unconsciously emulate the human she was impersonating.

She looked up at the stars. She had read books and seen films where people had used the stars to figure out where they were. She had not developed that ability, had never expected to need it. She recognised a pair of constellations – the Plough and Orion – but no others. Whether that meant she was close to home or far from home she couldn't say. She couldn't remember the last time she had looked up at the stars. If only she were able to use the stars to figure out how much time had passed since the episode over the English Channel... She felt in her heart that it had been no time at all, but she knew from her police work how loudly the heart can lie. And did she even have a heart at all? Who was she, and what was her purpose? Was she an impersonator, sent to assassinate someone, to infiltrate the police, completely unaware of her role she was to play?

She thought of the explosion that had killed the crystal dinosaur. Had that been a bomb, intended to kill? That didn't make sense. Impersonating a police officer is one thing: she might well end up in the company of important people, worthwhile targets. But a thief? Who would benefit from a robot impersonating her, and what robot could impersonate a thief well enough to pull off such a difficult robbery? And if they had both been robots back then, wasn't it rather a coincidence that they had ended up in a chase across the English Channel together?

After the dinosaur attack, just before Veronique had

woken up, a voice had talked about a secondary power source activating. Hence there must have been a primary power source that had been lost. The dinosaur must have bitten into it, causing the explosion. Beatrice smiled, happy that the dinosaur had been killed by its own greed.

Then, as if to berate her for such an ungracious thought, a bad thing happened. Though at first she didn't realise how bad it was.

It began with a series of soft little noises. She couldn't immediately identify them, which worried her, but they hardly seemed threatening. A rodent running through the undergrowth, perhaps? She peered into the darkness, wishing she had a torch. If this robot body had any additional senses, they were letting her down.

If it was some kind of rodent making the noises, there must be more than one. She could hear them coming from all over now, five from over here, five from over there. And she still couldn't see anything.

Unless...

Was that a cube silhouetted against the sky, sitting on that rock over there? That didn't look like a natural shape. She knew they hadn't left any equipment out: they had no equipment. She decided to wake Veronique.

"Veronique," she whispered. "Wake up."

She had spoken too quietly to wake Veronique, but loudly enough to provoke an angry murmur from whatever creatures were out there.

No more voices. She sneaked one hand over and gently rocked Veronique. Her new friend was a smart woman, and opened her eyes without making a noise. She knew Beatrice wouldn't have woken her mid-watch unless it was important. They made eye contact, bright eyes reflecting the moonlight, and Beatrice gently nodded to the new arrivals.

But it was one thing being awake and aware in the face of trouble, it was another to be able to do anything about it. Beatrice assumed that as robots they might have more strength than usual, though it hadn't been particularly apparent so far. Their strength might have been limited to allow them to pass more easily as humans; perhaps now the charade was over those shackles would fall away and they'd be ready to fight for their lives bare-handed. But perhaps not.

The least she could do was help Veronica back into a sitting position, and slowly she tried to do that. It turned the murmur in the darkness into distinct growling, and Beatrice prepared for attack.

"Come on then!" she shouted. "Let's see what you've got!"

Veronique had planned to issue her own challenge, but the words were arrested in her mouth by what happened next.

A hundred lights suddenly shone, from the ground all around, so bright the women could do nothing but close their eyes and squeeze them tight. Dazzled, a billion spots cascading across her vision, Beatrice tried to make sense of what she had seen in the fraction of a second before the light became too much.

But that couldn't be.

("When will you learn to stop saying that?" she asked herself sternly. "It clearly can.")

She was ready to open her eyes, and so was able to confirm what her brain had insisted she had seen. Lit from within by gems of all kinds, just like those they had seen within the dinosaur (though not, she now realised, after its body had fallen), topaz, amethyst, ruby, emerald, and many others, were a hundred or more tiny transparent boxes, cuboids. They were featureless, but Beatrice could have sworn they were all facing her. They were growling, a noise which seemed to be produced by a rattling of the crystals within the cuboids. Beside each of them was a small square patch of upturned turf. It looked like the odd noises she had heard had been these crystal cuboids popping up out of the ground.

"What the heck?" said Veronique. "Is it my birthday? Is this a dream?"

"After all the jewels you've stolen," said Beatrice, in an unkind tone she would later regret, "I suppose it's appropriate for them to get their revenge."

"They're not going to hurt us," said Veronique. These are little cuties!"

But she was wrong. Small crystalline arms formed on each side of the cuboids, and small crystalline legs lifted the cuboids up. They were ready to fight. Beatrice and Veronique braced themselves for death.

"Attack!" screamed the crystal cuboids in a single vibrato voice. They were implacable. They charged as one, giving Beatrice very little time to deal with each one as it reached her. The first few she kicked away to gain some space, but they were quickly on their way back. Their attacks were not powerful, but they were painful. Those arms and legs were little, but as any parent knows, even a punch from a little hand can hurt like billy-o if it catches you in the wrong place. From the gems the cuboids shot rays of flame, miniature versions of those the dinosaur had scorched her with. They didn't burn right through her clothes, but given time they ignited flames that had to be put out.

At least she could dodge. Poor Veronique couldn't even do that, and Beatrice could see her wincing as the beams hit her face and hands.

"Give up!" said an attacker who was crawling up the back of Beatrice's leg.

"Never!" she replied, snatching it up (it came away

with little shreds of her trousers in its tiny hands) and throwing it into the darkness.

"You cannot defeat us!" it said while still in the air.

"That's right!" said another crystal that was leaping on to her head from the overhanging rock. "Our crystal power is exceptional!"

She managed to get it off without losing too much of her hair, and looked around for anything that might give her an advantage against these deadly little beings.

The stretcher was no longer acting as any kind of cover, her jacket now burned through in a dozen places, so Beatrice decided to use it as a weapon. She grabbed the two branches and began to swing it around. It was like a baseball bat that gave you two chances to hit the ball. The crystal cuboids went flying left and right, but were soon scrambling back to the fight. She needed a more permanent solution.

She tried stamping on the cuboids but they were very tough and she became aware that the attempt was hurting her foot. Undeterred, she focused on the cuboids' arms and legs. That was more successful, and soon a dozen cuboids lay about her with arms snapped off and legs reduced to dust. But the crystals within continued to send their irritating little beams at her, and even as she kicked them away she could see that they were forming new arms and legs.

"Give up!" shouted a ruby cuboid. "Or we will slice you into strips with our crystal beams!"

Beatrice didn't stop fighting, but wanted to know what offer was on the table. "And if we do? If we stop fighting, what then?"

Her interlocutor was now spinning on the ground, its brief encounter with Beatrice having left it with just one leg. "We will slice you into strips with our crystal beams!"

"That doesn't..." – she paused to grab two cuboids

that had gotten perilously close to Veronique's face – "...sound like a very good deal." She smashed their legs together and threw them in the direction of the treeline. Maybe they would get stuck in there.

"It will save you all this pointless effort," said the ruby cuboid. "You can never defeat the wizard Gloaning!"

"Wizard?" said Beatrice with all the fatigue her body was feeling. "We don't care about defeating any wizard. We don't even believe in wizards."

"You destroyed her crystal dinosaur! You have invaded her island! You must die for your impertinence!" Its voice grew shriller and shriller, and she could see the ruby rattling around in the cuboid like a bluebottle in a jar. It gave her an idea.

"Yes I did," she declared, while trying to fight off three emerald and two topaz cuboids. She sobbed for breath. "I am the mightiest wizard of all England! I am here to bring your wizard low! We are your new crystal masters!"

"No! No! No! No!" The voice was so shrill, the ruby rattling so hard, that it cracked its own casing! Beatrice stamped upon the crack and the box ruptured, leaking clear fluid and leaving the ruby upon the ground, utterly inert.

"One down, hundreds to go!" shouted Beatrice with an enthusiasm that wasn't really hers.

"Well done!" said Veronique. "I can't do much to fight with my arms, but my voice is working fine. And I've never had much trouble winding people up."

It would be wrong to say that the battle turned at that point, because the cuboids were still arriving in uncountable numbers. But Beatrice and Veronique certainly began to get their licks in.

"The wizard is a pathetic power-obsessed idiot stuck in adolescence!" yelled Veronique. Crystals cracked their own cubes in anger, and Beatrice stamped down and kicked into the cracks.

"There are still too many," shouted Beatrice. "We're not making any space."

"Keep going," came Veronique's response. "We might get lucky." Her voice was raw from the effort of shouting out a half dozen insults per minute.

But while the ramped-up fury of the crystals helped Beatrice to fight them, it meant the creatures now fought with new ferocity. The little hands were no longer content to grab at trouser cloth. Their crystal fingers dug into her flesh like needles, and soon she was bleeding in a hundred places.

Then there was a moment when the crystal cuboids withdrew. The lights went out and for a moment there was silence. "Ha haaaa," shouted Veronique. "Does your cowardly crystal wizard want you back home to make her dinner?"

"Your little baby wizard!" is what Beatrice would have shouted in her turn had she not been too tired to speak. As it was she just leaned back against the rock and tried to get her breath back.

"You fought well," came the response. "But it is over."

Once the eyes of Beatrice and Veronique had had time to adjust to the darkness, the crystal lights flashed back on, dazzling them once again.

The cuboids charged.

Twenty of them hit Beatrice at once, and she knew it was indeed over. She felt beams burning into her skin in a dozen places, and once they had her eyes it would all be over. Somehow she found time to worry about Veronique, down there on the ground, but there wasn't a thing Beatrice could do to help her. A tear fell from her eye, then sizzled on her cheek. It had been evaporated by the burning beams of the crystal cuboids.

Time to die.

A shot rang out, followed by the sound of a shattering cube. Then another shot. And another.

The pressure on Beatrice lessened as cuboids turned to face this new threat. She took the risk of opening her eyes. They had been scrunched closed to keep them safe as long as possible. She had never quite given up all hope.

Cuboid shards were scattered on the ground, gems falling out into the mud. Cubes were exploding to left and right, even above her head. But who was doing the shooting? She couldn't see anyone. She took hold of the few crystal cuboids that were still clinging to her, and threw them up in the air – all were instantly blasted, and from the direction of the explosion Beatrice could tell where the shots were coming from.

Over there, on a rise, stood a figure. Only the silhouette of the upper body, head and hat was visible, the rest merging with the blackness of the night. Intermittent crystal beams sent in that direction lit up a pale, black-haired woman in a long black coat. However, the cuboids that sent those beams were destroyed so quickly that the illuminations were brief.

Beatrice turned to Veronique and picked up the few crystal cuboids that were still bothering her. By their light Beatrice could see that her friend had been hurt by their attacks, but her eyes seemed unhurt, and she seemed to be alive. Or functional? Was that the right word for a robot?

Few of the crystal cuboids were still active, and those that remained were burrowing back into the ground to escape. "We'll be back!" one of them screamed, before exploding into a thousand pieces after being hit with a bullet.

Beatrice sat down and waited for it to be over. It was important to gather her strength. This newcomer had helped them out of a difficult situation, but that didn't mean she was their friend. She might be a new enemy. Or an old enemy she hadn't yet recognised.

A few minutes later and the shooting was done. The cuboids were all gone, and the crystals lying on the ground seemed incapable of action without their transparent cuboid cradles. The silence was so loud it made Beatrice's ears ache.

The woman in the long dark coat came over to them. She didn't speak for a long moment, just looked at them, weighing them up, as if coming to a decision. Long black hair framed a narrow, angular face, and she wore glasses with thick black plastic rims. Her lips were pursed in what Beatrice guessed was a permanent pout of disappointment.

"Hello ladies," she said.

"Hello," said Veronique.

"Hello," said Beatrice. "Thank you for your help."

"My pleasure. Life is hard enough on this island, I hear, without those little devils bothering you." She reached into the deep folds of her coat and brought out a clear, flexible frame. Given a shake, it hardened into the shape of a stool, which she set on the floor. She swept her coat forward and sat down. "Would you like to introduce yourselves?"

Beatrice and Veronique looked at each other. What to do? Beatrice shrugged.

"I am Beatrice," she replied. "Or at least I think I am. I am an English police officer."

Veronique followed suit. "I call myself Veronique. She was chasing me because I'd stolen a very valuable item from the Queen."

The newcomer listened carefully, and nodded when they stopped speaking. "Go on."

"There was a storm," said Beatrice. "And then we woke up here. The jewel Veronique stole turned out to be the egg of a crystal dinosaur, which hatched and then tried to eat us."

"Did eat some of us," said Veronique, looking down to her waist.

The newcomer smiled, then got up and paced back and forth, kicking away the remains of the crystal cuboids and pressing the rubies, emeralds, amethysts and topazes down into the mud. Finally she returned to the two injured women and sat back down.

"My name is Cornelia Gilligan," she said. "Nothing else you know is true."

The Collection Agent

John Greenwood

As soon as he cut the engine, Bradley could hear only insects. He sat in the van, organising his papers, putting off the moment when he would have to leave the air-conditioned interior. He had parked in full view of the large bay windows. Let them look.

He held the fountain pen carefully so it would not spurt indigo onto his cream suit. There was still a smear of blood on the passenger seat. It shone a lustrous black against the leather. Bradley spat on another tissue and tried to mop it up. Again the tissue came away red.

When he could put it off no longer, Bradley stepped out onto finely raked gravel and locked the van. Hatless, he shielded his eyes with his hands. The air was thick with heat and the drone of insects. Every step into direct sunlight was a struggle.

He rang the doorbell, a plain worn nub set in concentric brass ripples. He waited. At least there was shade under the porch. Through a small square of frosted glass he saw vague movements and heard muffled footsteps coming downstairs. He hated the waiting. He turned away to take in the scenery. The road, the dry bushes, the soft curves of hills –

everything was covered in the same bone-yellow dust. Everything apart from the sky, which was a vast, harsh, cloudless blue. Tree ferns and banksias tumbled down the sloping garden to the road. Beyond that was empty land.

The door opened a little. Bradley saw a dark hallway, and an old man's face, thinning hair, a nose so bulbous and purple that it bordered on deformity. The old man wore a baggy vest and khaki shorts.

"I was having my siesta," said the man. He scratched a brown fold of stomach beneath the vest.

There was a reason why his employers insisted on the suit, Bradley thought to himself. It put the collection agent at a subtle advantage.

"Mr Felzer?" Bradley read the name from a clipboard, although he had read the case notes enough times to have memorised them.

The old man blinked. "Yes," he said. The face showed no emotion, but the shoulders sagged slightly. "I know who you are," he said.

"May I come in?" said Bradley brightly.

"Do I have a choice?" asked Felzer.

"You always have a choice, Mr Felzer. Of course, all choices entail consequences."

Felzer snorted. "Well put," he said. "I'm in the kitchen."

Bradley followed him down a dark corridor, noting the antique black telephone perched on its own table, and the framed prints of ships and seascapes.

"An interest in sailing?" he asked, padding his brow and the back of his neck with a clean handkerchief.

"A long time ago," said Felzer. He pushed through a curtain of orange plastic beads. "With my wife."

Bradley frowned. "Your wife?"

"Dead," said Felzer. "There's no-one else in the house."

Bradley parted the beads. The kitchen was a sorry

sight: a cooker, spattered with old oil; some withered houseplants in pots; walls shedding flakes of once-white paint; greasy linoleum on the floor; a table and two chairs, none matching. Felzer sat down.

"May I?" asked Bradley.

Felzer moved his fingertips across the yellow plastic table-top.

"Where's your friend?"

Bradley dragged out the other chair. "Who?"

"I thought you people always travelled in pairs."

Bradley sat down and put his briefcase flat on the table. "There was an accident," he said. "It's just me today."

"I was expecting two," said Felzer. He looked at the briefcase.

"Were you waiting for us?"

"No. Like I told you, I was having my siesta."

Bradley nodded. "Right."

He flicked the catches on the briefcase. Felzer jumped a little.

"Just a few preliminaries," said Bradley, taking a sheaf of forms from the briefcase. "Paperwork. Always the paperwork."

Felzer pursed his lips.

Bradley didn't believe a word of it about the siesta. The old man had been waiting, watching.

"Nice place you've got here," said Bradley, looking around the kitchen. A roller blind was drawn in the window, but daylight leaked in around the edges making a fuzzy square.

Felzer shrugged, tight-lipped, hands still dancing on the tabletop.

"Did you buy it with the contract money?"

Felzer nodded.

"Smart move," said Bradley. "You can't beat bricks and mortar."

Felzer sat there with his saggy stomach and long,

thin sunburnt arms. Bradley thought he looked like an orang-utang, a depressed, elderly ape. Through the arm hole of his vest Bradley saw wiry, white chest hairs and a shrivelled nipple. The old were so strange. Felzer's face was covered in lines, everywhere apart from the top of his head, which was a smooth, shiny dome, dotted with brown splodges. Bradley was reminded of a photo he'd once seen of Picasso. In Bradley's job he got to see quite a lot of old people, but he never quite got used to it.

"Not many people round here," said Bradley, taking the fountain pen from his pocket and carefully uncapping it. "This far south, I mean."

Felzer nodded.

"Was that why you chose it?"

"I used to have some neighbours," said Felzer.

"Oh?"

His face became pained, for a moment. "They moved away."

"The heat?"

"They didn't say."

Bradley didn't pursue that line any further.

He tried instead, "You have a lovely garden here."

Felzer shook his head, but there was a spark of interest.

"You should have seen it ten years ago," said Felzer, "when we could water now and then. That was a garden. The things that thrived here: lemons, bougainvillea, olive trees. We grew it all."

Bradley nodded, encouraging and smiling. "Very nice."

"All gone to rack and ruin now," said Felzer.

Bradley had his papers ready and pen poised. "Shall we get started?"

Felzer said, "Too hot, too dry. Hotter every year, now. No water. A lot of plants don't need much water, but they need a little. But there's none to spare."

"It's the same everywhere," said Bradley. "You're better off out of it. Nice and cool in here though, eh?"

Bradley looked around, taking in the greasy cooker, a calendar from two years ago pinned above it, the rust-streaked refrigerator door. Above them a ceiling fan gathered dust, long since fallen silent.

"I've spent most of the last three years in this room," said Felzer.

Taken by surprise, Bradley could only say, "Why?"

"Ran out of things to do. Where do you want me to sign?"

"You don't sign, I sign," said Bradley. "You already signed, when you took out the contract. I just have to certify that everything's been done fair and above board."

Felzer was looking him full in the face now. "Right."

"So if it's convenient, I'll get started on the tests."

Felzer laughed with his mouth only. "Convenient? Yes, it's convenient."

Bradley donned surgical gloves and took a fresh testing pack from the briefcase. He tore it open and laid the contents out in front of him on the table, each component in its own sterile plastic pouch: the handheld, the needles, the blood pressure cuff, the tools of his trade. There were one or two other items that he kept out of sight unless they were required.

He made Felzer hold out his forefinger, pricked it with a sterile needle, then fed the needle into a corresponding barrel in the handheld. He pressed the touch screen.

"Good. All clear."

"What is?" asked Felzer, still staring at him.

"That was the DNA test," explained Bradley. "To confirm your identity. We've had a few problems in the past. Mostly people trying to change their identity. They go into hiding, you know. But people have been known to hire a stooge. Can you believe that? A stand in. Usually somebody who doesn't quite understand what's going on. Otherwise why would they agree to it?"

"Why indeed?" said Felzer, his expression just the same.

Bradley took the man's blood pressure, examined his eyes with an opthalmoscope and confirmed that they weren't prosthetic. The handheld used ultrasound to detect the presence of two kidneys and two lungs. The tests lasted nearly an hour. When they'd finished, Bradley put all the instruments back in the briefcase and snapped it shut.

Felzer's expression changed. "Is that blood?" he said.

"Where?"

"On your briefcase."

"No," said Bradley, wiping the black plastic with the sleeve of his white shirt. It came away streaked with red.

Felzer said, "It is blood. Who does it belong to? Your last job?"

"Jesus, no. That would be totally unprofessional. In any case, we only usually do one job a day. This must be Raoul's blood."

Felzer stood up quickly, scraping his chair back, still staring at the blood on Bradley's sleeve.

"Who's Raoul?" he asked.

"My last partner," said Bradley. He tried to roll his sleeve up to hide the blood, but it showed in the creases. "I told you there was an accident."

"An accident?" Felzer shouted, gripping the back of the chair. "What sort of an accident? Where's Raoul?"

Bradley stood up too, and made calming gestures with the palms of his hand as though he were gently pressing the tension back down. "It doesn't matter," he said, before revising that to, "Raoul's dead."

Felzer narrowed his eyes, then started to smile. The man was actually smiling.

"It doesn't matter? A man is dead and you say it doesn't matter? I don't like this," he said. "I don't like it one little bit. Something funny is going on here. I think maybe we should call somebody. I'm going to make a call."

He started edging crabwise towards the bead curtain.

"I'll tell you if you like," said Bradley.

Felzer stopped and turned around on the threshold.

"I didn't want to burden you with it," Bradley went on. "Not at a time like this. I didn't think you'd want to hear about it. But if you do, then I'll tell you. I'll tell you the whole thing."

"So tell me," said Felzer.

"We were attacked by bandits," said Bradley.

Felzer stared, not moving from the doorway. "That's bullshit," he said, examining the undulating orange waves of beads as they slipped across his hands.

"It's true. They had motorbikes. Souped-up choppers and stuff. And shotguns. They shot Raoul. He didn't make it. I had to leave him behind."

"I didn't see any marks on your van," said Felzer.

"They surrounded the van. I was in the back, getting some sleep. They must have made Raoul get out, at gunpoint. It was the shot that woke me. I shouted for Raoul, but he didn't answer. I could hear voices outside. There was no way of knowing what was going on out there – there are no windows in the back of those vans, you know? I had to try and crawl into the cab without being spotted."

Felzer had moved back into the kitchen. He sagged down into the other chair and started drumming on the table-top again with his brown fingers.

"Did they see you?"

"No, not then. There's a kind of rolling screen between the cab and the back of the van. I pushed it up just a foot or so, very slowly, and wriggled through.

I was hunched down under the steering wheel, The driver's side door was open where Raoul must have got out, but all I could see was the road. At least I knew we were still on a road. I had no idea where.

"I heard someone saying, 'Check his wallet. Check it again.' Then another man's voice said, 'Got it. Fuck, those shotguns make a mess.' I guessed that Raoul was either dead or badly wounded. In a moment they would be coming to look inside the van, probably to steal it. Probably that's why they made Raoul get out – they didn't want to mess up the interior."

Felzer nodded. "So what did you do?"

"As soon as I heard that talk about shotguns, I got my gun out."

Felzer sat upright. "I didn't know you people carried guns."

"For emergencies only," said Bradley. "The key was missing from the ignition. I figured they'd taken it from Raoul. I fished my own key out of my pocket, but what was I supposed to do? Just drive off? I was hunkered down there on the floor, trying to think, when I saw a leg appear in the gap where the door was open. Without thinking I jumped into the driver's seat, swung my legs around and kicked the door open. The whole thing took no longer than a second. I heard the door hit something, then it slammed back shut. My foot was already on the accelerator when I looked out of the driver's window and saw a guy laid out on the ground. All in black leather, sunglasses, big old beard. I jammed my foot to the floor. It was like my leg just went into some sort of spasm. Some other guys had to dive out of the way. I don't think I hit anybody. Some parked bikes got mashed up. I don't feel bad about that – I mean, they had killed Raoul. But the side of the van got scraped up pretty badly. I'm going to have some explaining to do when I get back to the office."

While Bradley talked, Felzer got up, reached down an old cigar tin from a high shelf, and took out a cigar. He unwrapped the cellophane tube. A good sign, thought Bradley. These little rituals, small indulgences saved up for the end – they were on safer ground now. Even so, Bradley was a little disappointed that Felzer hadn't saved one for him. He'd known previous clients do things like that. There were some very genuine people out there. Really nice, ordinary folks who'd made their choice, signed their contract, and learned to live with it. Felzer wasn't one of those. He may have been ordinary once, he may have even have been nice, but now he was a long way from either. Sometimes the ink from that contract leaked into people's veins. Once you allowed that poison in, the rest of your time, whatever you hadn't sold off, was tainted. It had happened to Felzer. He had allowed it to happen.

"You been saving that for today?" asked Bradley, as the old man fired up the cigar.

Felzer shook his head, puffing meticulously to keep the coal glowing. "No, I just remembered it was there."

"Just the one left, eh? Lucky that."

Felzer just said, "What happened to Raoul? You didn't just leave him there?"

"What else could I do?" said Bradley. "There was a whole gang of them. Thirty, maybe forty armed guys against me with my little pistol. No thanks."

Felzer sucked at the cigar, seeming to regain his composure with each exhalation of blue smoke.

"Didn't they try and shoot you as you drove off?" he asked.

"Sure they did. I guess I was lucky."

"I'd call that more than luck," said Felzer. "I'd call that a fucking miracle."

He was staring at Bradley again through the curling smoke. He looked like he was restraining himself from pushing the cigar into Bradley's eye. He puffed and puffed until Bradley could barely see his face.

"I guess you're right," said Bradley. "A miracle, really."

"And they didn't come after you either?" said Felzer.

"No," said Bradley. "I thought it was strange at the time. But they didn't."

Felzer asked, "Did you call the police?"

"What police? There are no cops within a hundred miles of here. They wouldn't come this far south. We are in the middle of a desert, in case you'd forgotten."

"I hadn't. They used to grow grapes around here, you know. It used to be called France."

"Well they don't anymore," said Bradley. "They don't grow anything. We drove over eight hundred miles without seeing a single living soul, until those bandits caught up with us. Why would anyone want to live here?"

"We were looking for peace and quiet," said Felzer.

"And did you find it?"

"The latter."

Bradley had never liked cryptic answers, nor the sort of clever, dishonest men who made them. Felzer was playing for time. He would talk about anything to postpone the inevitable for a few more minutes.

Bradley stood up, removed his coat and hung it on the back of the chair. Then he clicked open the briefcase again. "I think we're ready to begin," he said.

Felzer didn't move. "So soon?" he said.

"Actually no," said Bradley, taking a roll of tightly scrunched white plastic from the case. "We're late. It took us a long time to locate you, even with the GPS tracking. Strictly speaking, we should have done this two months ago. But you already knew that, didn't you? The collection date is written on your contract."

"I haven't looked at it for years. In fact I'm not even sure where it is now. Are you sure about that date? I thought I had at least another six months."

Bradley had heard all this before. "I've got a copy right here." He slid a sheet from the briefcase and laid it on the table in front of the old man. He stabbed the date with his forefinger. "Right there, Mr Felzer. And that's real paper."

"Let me look at this," said Felzer, squinting at the document.

"Be my guest," said Bradley. "I'll just get set up over here."

The contract stated that the contractee, Mr Alfred Felzer, agreed to sell twenty-five years of his estimated life expectancy, in exchange for a payment of $300,000. Clients could choose to sell however many years they wanted, but twenty was the minimum. Payment was on a sliding scale: a non-smoking teetotaller with no family history of serious congenital illness could expect to get $200,000 by agreeing to die at 60 rather than an estimated 80. But $200,000 didn't buy much nowadays. For each year of your fifties you got $20,000. This went up to $50,000 a year for your forties, and shot up to $100,000 for each year of your thirties. Nobody under 30 was legally allowed to sign up.

The money was paid out as an annuity. Felzer had opted for a typical package: twenty-five years of his life-expectancy had netted him $300,000. That was more money than Bradley expected to earn in a lifetime of service to the company.

Felzer shook his head. "No, that can't be right. There must have been a mistake. I think you should go back and talk to your boss about this: there's been some sort of administrative error here."

Bradley activated a small button on the roll of plastic. There was a hissing sound that went on and on. Slowly the plastic baton began to unroll and inflate.

"No need," he said. "That's all been checked out beforehand. There's no mistake, Mr Felzer."

Felzer pointed. "What's that?"

"Self-inflating stretcher," said Bradley. "Wonderful invention. Made our lives so much easier." He put the stretcher down on the dirty linoleum, pushed the chairs and table out of the way and turned away from Felzer to his briefcase. He snapped open a clean hypodermic needle.

"Am I supposed to lie down on that?" asked Felzer. His voice was very quiet and hoarse now like he was having trouble speaking.

"That's the general idea," said Bradley.

"I'd rather sit."

"I need you to lie down, Mr Felzer," said Bradley, keeping his back turned while he readied the needle. "We don't want you falling over and banging your head."

"What will it matter?" said Felzer, and then, "Oh, of course – you don't want to damage the goods."

"That's one way of putting it."

Bradley capped the needle and stowed it in his pocket as he always did. Usually he had Raoul to keep the client calm and pliant.

The stretcher was almost fully inflated. Bradley crouched to smooth out a couple of wrinkles, then stood up and looked at Mr Felzer. The old man was standing against the wall with his hands behind his back, as though afraid of the stretcher itself. It was not an unusual reaction.

"It's quite comfortable," said Bradley.

"Who will get my – my organs?"

"Whoever can afford them."

The job was nearly over now. Bradley just wanted to get it over with and get out.

"You'll make a big profit out of them, I suppose."

"Me personally? No, I don't work on commission, Mr Felzer. But we are operating a business, so naturally there is mark up. How much depends on the condition of the products. We won't know that until later."

"You're going to cut me up?"

"Not me. I'm just the collection agent."

Bradley had allowed the conversation to drift into dangerous territory. The client was showing symptoms of extreme stress: sweating, shaking, stammering. None of this would have happened had Raoul been around.

"Are there any religious or secular rituals you'd like me to perform before completion?" asked Bradley. "I notice that you didn't specify any in the original contract, but you are entitled to change your mind at this point."

Felzer shook his head impatiently. "Nothing like that."

"In that case, we're all set," said Bradley. He remembered not to rub his hands together – Raoul had told him to avoid this. "Just lie down and make yourself comfortable. Your head goes at this end."

Felzer clamped his mouth shut and carried on shaking his head like he didn't know how to stop.

"Lie down, Mr Felzer," said Bradley.

"I can't go through with it," said Felzer. "I just can't." He said it over and over again.

"Mr Felzer, you have signed a legally binding contract. My company has fulfilled its part by paying you the agreed sum."

"I'll pay you back," said Felzer.

"Even if that were permitted by the terms of the contract, you don't have the money."

"I can get it for you. I'll sell the house. We could make a private arrangement, just between you and me. You can have the house. You can have everything."

None of this was new to Bradley. People would offer anything, do anything, to get out of contract completion. He'd heard some tall stories from the other collection agents. He didn't know if they were true. This bargaining had to be stopped. The trouble was, when you were dealing with a man like Felzer, in his position, there was no point in appealing to his moral dignity.

Bradley said, "You have nothing that I want. And who would buy this house in the middle of a desert, a bandit-infested desert? Nobody, that's who. Now, I need you to lie down."

"There are no bandits here," said Felzer.

"Lie down on the stretcher."

"There are no bandits. You're full of it. All that stuff about bandits. It's all bullshit."

"It's not bullshit, Mr Felzer," said Bradley. "But it is irrelevant."

"Where did that blood come from?" said Felzer.

"What blood?"

"The blood on your briefcase."

They stood on either side of the stretcher which took up half the length of the kitchen.

"What are we talking about?" said Bradley.

"You said it was Raoul's blood," said Felzer. "You said that Raoul was dead."

"That's right, I did."

He took a sidestep towards his coat, still draped over the chair. He could have done with Raoul's help. The job was threatening to go sour.

Felzer smiled oddly. "You said they made him get out of the car before they shot him. So how did his blood get on your briefcase?"

Bradley shrugged and took another sidestep. He was within reach of his jacket. "How the hell should I know? I panicked. You heard what happened back there. I drove off like a madman. I probably cut myself on the edge of the door or something."

"You didn't cut yourself," said Felzer.

"Mr Felzer, I am going to ask you for the last time to lie down."

"You can't make me do anything I don't want to."

"I am a registered collection agent, and as such I am empowered by law to use any necessary force to ensure compliance with all terms of the contract signed by my employer."

He was about to say, "You leave me no choice," when he noticed the expression on Felzer's face and his gun in Felzer's fist.

"You know that only takes tranquilliser darts," said Bradley, but instinctively he put his hands up when the barrel was pointed at him.

Felzer said, "Shall we find out?" He jabbed the barrel of the gun at Bradley, and watched as the collection agent flinched.

"Stay here," he said.

Bradley didn't move and kept his hands above his head. He said, "Where are you going to go?"

Felzer just looked at him, then walked backwards down the hall and went out of the front door, closing it quietly after him. Bradley heard him trying the locked doors on the van. He half-expected Felzer to come back for the keys, but he never did. Instead all was quiet. Bradley stood alone in the gloom of the kitchen, listening to the insects outside, letting his eyes rest on the faded calendar, the burnt coffee pot on the sticky stove, the cups and plates in the sink, shadows dancing on the grey walls. All that money, and this was what was left. Twenty-five years of taking it easy.

Then he strode down the hall and banged open the front door. The sunlight was blinding and the midday heat made him gasp. When his eyes had adjusted he looked to the horizon and saw a tiny figure running away across a dusty yellow hill. He got in the van, backed it carefully down the steep drive, then gunned the engine before accelerating through the fence that ran along the side of the road. The barbed wire snapped like guitar strings. In a second he was bumping over parched hillocks dotted with tufts of grass. He kept his eyes on the running figure. Felzer stopped, turned around and fired the gun at the approaching vehicle. The shot went yards wide. Bradley kept driving at him. Next time Felzer waited until the van was in range before firing again. The dart skidded across the windscreen.

"That's right," said Bradley. "Keep that up."

He kept back until Felzer had emptied the gun. Bradley's only worry was that Felzer would try to shoot his tyres out, but the idea never occurred to the old man. Bradley saw him toss the empty weapon aside and carry on running, stumbling over tussocks of dry grass. Bradley put his foot down. In a minute he was driving alongside the old man, very slowly. He wound down the passenger's side window.

"Stop," he shouted, but Felzer carried on running. Bradley wondered whether he was going to have a heart attack. His face was red and he was limping along, arms flailing. Would that reduce his commission? He couldn't remember anything like this happening to him before. Felzer just would not give up. He was barely upright now, stumbling over the rough ground, hunched over with pain and breathlessness. He fell, but caught himself with the palms of his hands and ran on, almost on all fours.

Bradley stopped the van, but left the engine running. He allowed himself a moment, then opened the driver's door and jumped down onto the baked hard earth. He could feel the heat through the soles of his shoes.

Felzer had not got far. It was a short, hot sprint for Bradley. He tripped Felzer up from behind and the man's knees buckled easily. He fell face forward into the dust, breathing in ragged gasps. Bradley knelt on his back, pulled his arms behind his back and cuffed him with a cable-tie.

"Let me sit up at least," said Felzer.

With some difficulty Bradley rolled the man onto his back then pulled him into a sitting position. Sweat ran down Felzer's face, making trails in the dust on his face. When he could speak, he said, "Well, I gave you a run for your money, didn't I? At least I did that."

"You did," said Bradley. He fished the hypodermic, still capped and ready, from his pocket.

"Are we ready now?" said Bradley. He knelt down on the ground facing the old man, and examined the needle, making sure it was still intact.

"Almost," said Felzer. "I haven't run so hard since I was a young boy." He grinned. Blood welled up from his lip.

He shouted out something without words. The sun beat down on them both.

"Is that what you needed to do?" asked Bradley. "Is that enough?"

Felzer's eyes were on the horizon. "No. It's never enough," he said.

Bradley leaned forward to grip the man's upper arm, the needle ready in his other hand. At the same time that he saw the front wheel of the motorcycle, Bradley felt something hard pressed against the back of his head. Motorcycles were drawing in to form a tight circle around them. The man behind him holding the gun said, "Okay, Mr Felzer?"

"Yes, thank you," said Felzer. "Never better."

Bradley turned around. A man's face, bearded, with dark glasses and an ugly red welt down one side of his face, looked down at him. Another man cut the cable tie and helped Felzer to his feet.

"You wanted to know what I did with the money," said Felzer.

Bewildered, Bradley looked around. Men laughed, lounging against their parked bikes. The needle was snatched from Bradley's hand. A moment later, Felzer was brandishing it.

"Well," he said, "was that enough for you?"

Contractual Obligations

Howard Watts

The intercom's buzzing distracted him from the report. He laid the papers to his right and thumbed the desk button.

"Minister, a visitor. PPD, immediate attention, PM's signature on all forms."

He sighed, peering over the rim of his bifocals towards the door. "Cancel my two o'clock, Maxine. Send them in – tea in five, please."

The heavy oak panelled door set into the centre of the opposite wall opened silently. The minister watched as the visitor closed the door behind him, then slowly approached the vacant brown leather captain's chair.

Placing his elbows upon the desk, clasping his fingers together to rest his chin upon them, the minister sighed again. A Parliamentary Pass Down, on a Monday afternoon? Unprecedented.

As the figure momentarily found the light from the Georgian windows behind the desk, the minister frowned. It was certainly not the weather for such attire – a Crombie hat, Burberry scarf, aviator sunglasses and grey trench coat? His guest sat slowly, almost with difficulty. The minister's lack of definitive observational conclusions regarding his visitor caused him concern. It was after all a rather heavy lunch, he decided, defending himself as the captain's chair creaked, blaming his lack of decision on indigestion.

The figure remained motionless for a minute, before reaching inside their coat with a black leather glove. A sepia coloured envelope found the sunlight between the two men as it was offered across the desk. Taking it, the minister placed it to his left as his guest spoke.

"You're new."

A statement, the minister decided, delivered with a hint of condescension, finally relieved he'd concluded something about this PPD. He cleared his throat. "No, no I'm afraid you're mistaken," he began with a slight self-satisfied smile. "I've held this position for almost thirty-five years."

His guest remained unmoved by the apparent correction, causing the minister's eyes to narrow with disappointment.

"You're new."

Definite this time, most certainly. Such a superior, judgemental, mocking air. He answered quickly. "If aware of my position then you'll understand my time is limited. Why are you here, mister?"

His guest pointed to the envelope, stabbing a finger upon it once.

The minister picked it up, carefully pulling out the pages to lay them before him. Adjusting his bifocals, he rested his forearms along the edge of his desk, scanning the documents. Nodding to himself he smiled openly.

His guest spoke. "Our arrangements have been altered, contrary to our contract." The voice was mid-ranged, even, but strained, slow, as if each syllable required great effort from the struggling larynx and tongue.

"Mm. As I understand it," said the minister placing the pages back into the envelope, "our representative delivered the proposed change of contract documentation, and was summarily eaten?" He looked up, waiting for a reaction, offering the envelope back, the summer afternoon's sunlight highlighting disturbed flecks of circulating dust around it.

His guest removed his hat, placing it upon his lap. He uncurled the scarf carefully, folding it into a pad and placing it into the upturned hat. He removed his sunglasses, snapping the arms closed to lay them onto the scarf before dropping the hat upon the minister's desk. He leant forward into the sunlight, and an odour of evergreen found the minister's nose as his guest snatched the envelope back, placing it on the desk between them.

"My name is Mr Unus. I regret your representative's treatment – understandable considering the circumstances. My brethren grow impatient. Hunger clouds their behaviour, an impatient and angered hunger I've focused upon for centuries to abate, to keep you 'limiteds' safe. Be clear, at this time I have no desire for them to stagger back into your civilisation, to ravage it as before."

"Your settlement is fortunate to exist, following the outbreak and subsequent cull of 2018."

Unus shook his head with an audible creak as his atlas and axis bones ground together.

"Genocide," he rasped, "The outbreak was beyond my control, hence our contract – our compliance is on record, and forms part of such?"

A question this time, decided the minister, raising his eyebrows with a grin. Sitting back in his chair he removed his bifocals, closing his eyes, rubbing the bridge of his nose with thumb and forefinger as he picked out a passage from the contract to recite from memory. "*Your disease eradicates all others. Detailed study of test subjects from the settlement will ascertain how your bodies remain active after death. Once the genetic trigger is identified and isolated, it can perhaps be used to eradicate our own debilitating and fatal diseases, Alzheimer's, cancer..."*

"Understood and not in question," interrupted Unus. "Our food supply has ended. Without sustenance we cannot offer new test subjects. Without feasting our bodies cannot return to what they once were, human once again, a thousand years on. What has become of the source we agreed? What has become of our ultimate salvation?"

The minister sat forward a little and replaced his bifocals, folding his arms across his chest. "RTA. The eighteen-wheeler overturned in bad weather en route to you. Bodies were found, identified at the scene, some still tagged. Relatives want to know why their dearly departed were piled together with a handful of convicted criminals, after they'd supposedly been cremated, in the back of..."

"Your complications are not our concern, simply your lack of competence and compliance."

"The accident established a paper trail," replied the minister, raising his voice slightly. "Witnesses, surviving criminals' statements were taken." He nodded to the report at his right. "This whole sorry affair leads to my door, which will lead finally to yours. A comprehensive investigative team has been assembled."

"You fear their attention, rather than ours?"

He shrugged. "I fear neither."

"As I stated, our compliance is on record. I have written your history books for you as I have witnessed it. Five centuries of truths, while I and my kind cowered, until used by your kind during your last war, to reduce the enemy of these shores to bones. None remained that mattered, none were turned to our way. We fulfilled our contractual obligations during those times – afford us the same, now."

The minister clasped his hands together, placing

them upon the desk before him. "There's nothing I can do, I'm afraid."

Unus smiled, a wide red and bone white yawn of decay. "Your envy of us, the *'Immortalibus Mortuos'* as one wartime PM once called us, is obvious. We remain, we see the future while you struggle to avoid your inevitable decay to dust. Your time is limited, ours limitless. We will see the end of this earth, mankind will not. We're unsoiled compared to *Homo sapiens*, free of your lies, your betrayals, murder, your wars. You prey on practically every species walking this earth, while we only crave one, to survive, to nourish and reverse decay and rejuvenate us, to co-exist – as agreed, at a price to us both, as per the contract."

"Mr Unus, you must understand – these are difficult times, different people are involved now, as you've noticed. They want answers then, ultimately, change. Hiding your settlement, the roads leading to it, erasing orbital satellite data, it all costs taxpayers' money, and the costs are escalating each year."

"Change, cost? Your taxpayers would prefer history to repeat itself, for us to feast upon London, once more? Can you afford another fire, of a greater magnitude to that which devastated the capital in its attempt to eradicate us, almost four hundred years ago? Your hedonistic depredations have all but destroyed your precious civilisation, in the name of change." He stabbed his finger once more upon the contract, leaning forward into the light. "You need us all, yet just *one* of us could end you all." His grin stretched grey skin across black molars, broken tendons of brown and crimson flapping behind bone. "This one remains," he said, nodding with satisfaction, "hidden beyond our settlement, one that can be called upon to act for us if this contract is not honoured."

The minister exhaled slowly. "I fully understand. I'll

make the necessary arrangements, immediately. Your supplies will continue."

Unus stood as Maxine entered, pushing a cart of clinking bone china. "Then our meeting is at a close. I trust I'll not need to make a further appointment to this office, during your remaining tenure?" He slowly picked up the envelope, sliding it beneath his coat.

The minister shook his head, thinking quickly. "The investigative team will follow due procedure. Expect them at your door by the end of this week." He looked up into dead eyes. "Consider them an entrée, preceding your next delivery."

Unus nodded once, picking up his hat as Maxine placed a cup and saucer upon the desk.

"Contractual obligations will resume. Good day, minister."

The minister was already pouring a cup of tea, refusing to look up to his departing guest. "Good day, Mr Unus."

I Couldn't See Past the Spider

Stephen Theaker

---

1. I Couldn't See Past the Spider

It was large and blocking most of my view. It hadn't moved for more than three hours. What was it doing there? What was its particular fascination with the space immediately in front of my eyes? The rest of the room surely held interest for spiders. There was a multitude of nooks and crannies, dark spaces in which it could usefully have occupied itself, or at least I assumed that there were, but no, it did not budge.

And of course the other side of the problem was that I was unable to move my head. Or any other part of my body. So I was at the mercy of the eight-legged lack-a-care.

Was it sleeping? Do spiders sleep? Now, from a vantage of safety, I could perhaps discover the answer, but then I could not. I tried to tell if its eyes were open, but I had no idea what they would look like if they were closed, or even if they would ever close.

Spiders, eh?

I tried to blow it away, but the strength I could lend to the gust was too feeble. It merely rustled its hairs.

The spider did not even turn to face me. Maybe it did not need to – do spiders have three hundred and sixty degree vision?

Every so often one of its legs would twitch, ever so slightly, but despite my fervent prayers to Thirdle, my favourite of all the imaginary beings that lurk behind the curtain, it did not shift its stance.

All I could see of the room beyond the spider was a wall or two, covered in orange hessian. There was little light, just enough to let me see the spider, but it seemed to be natural light, so presumably there was a window in the room. During my three hours of wakefulness the light had neither waxed nor waned, so I guessed the time to be somewhere in the early afternoon.

Stumped by the problem presented by the spider, my mind turned to other issues. How had I got here?

I had no answer.

The last thing I remembered...

I realised that I did not remember anything at all.

My name. At least I must know that?

No, even that escaped me.

Signs pointed towards a bang on the head, then, an abduction in the night! Perhaps someone had taken me from somewhere. It wasn't much, but it was a start. Okay, so it wasn't even a start, but it was at least a provisional hypothesis on which basis I could proceed.

Back to the spider, then. I tried blowing again, harder this time, now I suspected I was in danger. My hypothesised kidnappers might soon return! Still nothing. The alien thing crouched there, engaged in its monstrous thoughts of liquefied flies and swinging from webs.

Another aspect of the problem then. Why couldn't I move? I tried my arms again – nothing. They weren't senseless, though, or numb. They just wouldn't move. Perhaps they had been tied so long that they could no longer feel the bonds, in the same way that if a lover lays a hand upon your back and does not move it, you lose awareness of it until it moves again. I decided to give it my all. Three hours of lying on the floor like this and only now were my thoughts clearing enough to give me the determination to succeed!

I took a deep breath and threw all my energy into lifting my arms.

There, that was something! I didn't feel my arms rise, but I felt them hitting the floor when they fell.

I began to revise my hypothesis. Perhaps, rather than a bang on the head, I had been drugged! Then dumped on the floor in my captor's lair.

But I still could not see past the spider. I stuck my tongue out at it.

What was that? It moved! The spider moved, ever so slightly in my direction!

Of course, that only worsened my problem, in that it now blocked even more of my vision, and I was able to see its hard black shell in additional appalling detail. Its eyes, or at least half of them, stared at me with what I imagined to be amused cruelty. Or was it patience, the patience of a hunter?

And what was its prey?

My tongue? My teeth?

I stuck my tongue out at it again. Once more it moved – in fact it sprang! Thankfully out of my vision! Not so thankfully, onto my tongue! There was no option but to crush the beast against the roof of my mouth and swallow it whole, hoping that a second of pain would repay the beast for three hours of torture. It was a small victory, you might think, but one that left me happy, if slightly nauseous.

I was now able to see much more of the room in which I was held. All three walls in my view were covered in the same orange material, while the ceiling laboured under the weight of woodchip encrusted paper that had been painted green. Clearly this room was not the work of the Decorator Kings of Akk-Shabar!

I held that thought – it was the first to have taken me beyond the walls of this room, intellectually if not physically. It seemed my memories were beginning to return. I noted this with a smile, then continued my consideration of the room.

The window, if such it was, was still not visible to me (nor was a door), but the lack of shadows suggested it was covered, light drizzling in from behind a heavy curtain.

There were just three objects in the room beside myself. A jug, a bowl, and a table upon which the jug and bowl stood.

Seeing them, I realised that I was both hungry and thirsty; the spider disposed of, I now had a new quest!

I moved my arms once again; this time I felt them lift, and fall. I did it again, this time with enough force to roll myself over. The drug – or perhaps it had been a spell? – was on its way out of my system!

And now I could see whence the light came. It was a slatted door, and through its slats I could see a thick sheet, probably draped to conceal the entrance from curious eyes.

Did that mean someone would be looking for me? Did I have friends? A name tried to find its way to the tip of my tongue, but stubbornly held back, dismayed I imagine by the evidence of the spider's demise. Sam, Sal, Sax? It would come to me later. I trusted in my recovering mind to bring me the information when it was ready.

Having succeeded in moving my arms, I now found I could also move my head, though it had little practical application now that the spider was gone. I rolled it around a little to test for evidence of a bump, but found nothing.

Legs, then. I tried to shake them, and was successful at the third attempt. With huge effort I was able to curl them up and push off from the wall. I did it gently, so as not to make a noise. Then I pushed again, this time against the floor, then once more, and this time brought my head close to the table. I used my feet to turn myself around, then hooked them under the table and slowly, slowly, ever so slowly, for fear of upsetting the jug, I pulled myself up to a sitting position. The muscles in my belly screamed at this unexpected demand, but did their duty.

I felt I had won. Of course there was still much more to do. But wow, I had really come a long way. The spider no longer blocked my view, my arms and legs were now working, and I was mere spans away from food and drink. I could not yet see the contents of the jug, but the bowl contained the fruits of the mungan tree, both the yellow and burgundy varieties. My awakening brain reminded me that burgundy mungans were remarkably expensive at this time of year, indicating that my captor was both well-off and generous towards his guests, willing or otherwise. I began to imagine their wonderful juices filling my mouth, pouring down my throat, and then ruined it by wondering how the flavours would be affected by the spider's aftertaste. That damned spider continued to vex me! Never mind: if there was ample water in the jug I could swill and spit before eating the fruit.

My arms were still behind my back, but now I had a marvellous view of my legs and feet. They were bound at the ankles and knees, not by ropes from which I could have wriggled, or chains that would have rendered escape utterly impossible, but by words. They swept around and around my knees and ankles, never actually touching them, but not allowing them the space to separate. Words such as "binding", "tether" and "connect", holding me tight. In amongst them I saw a name, surely the signature of he who had bound me fast in this way: Fellegrin. The name was unfamiliar, but, as my happily compliant brain let me know, he must have been a mighty user of magic for the spell to persist for so long in his absence. That I was now able to move indicated that it had weakened, in particular around my head, freeing both my mind and my neck, but few could have made it last even so long.

What to do now? If I waited the spell would weaken further, and my escape would be eased. On the other hand, this Fellegrin would be aware of his spell's duration of efficacy and would in all likelihood return to restore its strength; for all I knew this process had already happened in the past. My memory was not yet fully returned; I might have tried to escape many times before, only to have my memories of each attempt blithely washed away by Fellegrin, the dastard.

There was no option, I had to try to escape now. But first, to my feet, and then to eat and drink. I curled my legs up again, managing this time to get them underneath myself; I kneeled up, and put my face to the jug, only to gasp at an unexpected aroma: Poosol, the favourite wine of the southern cities! This was a treat not to be missed, even if intoxication should impede my escape! After a moment's thought on procedure, I grasped the jug firmly between my teeth and gently raised it into the air. Disaster! Even as the merest trickle found its way to my eager lips the jug slipped, and fell to the floor, shattering into one hundred and thirty-seven pieces (I surprised myself by being able to count them so quickly) and spilling its wonderful contents onto the floor.

I considered throwing myself after it to lick up the remains – I was after all very thirsty, and Poosol was after all very delicious – but restrained myself. If I am honest, it was only because I suspected the noise of the crash would attract the attention of my jailers, and I refused to sacrifice my dignity to those who had stolen my freedom. That I now knelt in a pool of wine was embarrassing enough.

I contented myself by leaning forward to bite from the burgundy mungan. It was as sumptuous as I had dreamed, the taste so rich that it washed away all thoughts and flavours of spiders, in fact washing away all thought of escape, at least for a second or two. I took another bite, and then another, only at the fourth deigning to sample the more common yellow variety.

No one came to investigate the noise, which raised my spirits considerably. Perhaps there was a chance of escape, after all. I ate lots more, simultaneously letting my strength build and my bonds weaken. For the first time I began to hope for something beyond a drink and a chance to stretch my legs.

There were fewer words now, and their strength had declined. They said things like "inconvenience", "bother" and "irritate", so I decided to test them. Success! My arms and legs separated, the odd word still flying from one limb to another, but a good third of them falling illegibly to the ground. The rest did little but drag at me as I threw the remaining unbitten fruits into my pocket and quickly gobbled as much as I could of the rest.

Then to the door!

I tried it gently, but with no luck: it was locked, though I could see no trace of a keyhole. Bringing my eye to one of the slats I saw a whirl of words between door and covering curtain: "block", "obscure" and "baffle". Nothing I couldn't handle, and perhaps they were to thank for concealing my accident with the jug! I leaned back and kicked at the door. The door did not move but three of the slats fell. I pulled at more, making enough room to work my way through. In seconds I was through to the other side.

A rough-looking fellow dozed drunkenly (the heavy snores and thick odour gave the game away) in a worn armchair in a corner. I thought briefly about waking him for interrogation – or revenge! – but thought better of it and decided to make a clean escape if possible. For all I knew there would be other guards in other rooms.

However, there were not, and soon I was out on the street, wondering which city I was in and how I would discover my own identity. My problems were many, but so were my options. I had discovered myself to have a pleasingly optimistic outlook, and it made me smile.

2. The Slow Communication

I wandered through the city, looking for something to spark a memory, wondering if I would recognise Fellegrin if I saw him, wondering if there was a way to stop him from recognising me. A disguise would be useful (how much so I did not know – could it fool such as he?) but what I really needed was information.

The streets bustled with light brown men and women wrapped in colourful cloths; glancing at my arm for confirmation I saw my shade was lighter, but was clearly not so unusual as to attract attention, since not a one of them so much as glanced at me. My clothes, I now realised, were slightly dirtied from my time on the floor. No one was throwing stones to chase me out of the city, but none saw me as a person of interest, one who might be persuaded to part with money for their goods. That had to change; no one would give me information unless they thought I had something to offer in return.

I found a nice place to sit, just off the town square, a nook with a wall from where I could see the market traders and their customers, without being too obvious to passers-by. I chewed on a mungan, taking immense pleasure in its unfathomably luminous effects upon my palate, while encouraging my thinkpot to give up more of its secrets. It was interesting that no one had commented on the words that still flew on occasion around my head: perhaps I was in some manner sensitive to them, while others were not. That could be one clue to my history. I searched my clothes for others, unsuccessfully. If these were my clothes, I had been a dull man indeed. Even discounting the grime, they were plain and functional, with not a thing to suggest the flair and exuberance I felt already to be an integral part of my personality. The pockets, save for a few remaining mungans, were empty, as one might expect of a prisoner's pockets. I began to suspect that these were not my clothes, that these had perhaps been applied to my person without my conscious approval. It was the only possibility that made sense, since my dislike of them increased with every word that fell from its orbit around my head.

Stealing was not an option. From my vantage point as the afternoon drew on I saw one, two and then three thieves apprehended as they tried to do their dishonest business. Each lost a finger on the spot, clipped to the third knuckle by a city guard. Despite the apparent affluence of this city, that thieves even tried under threat of such retribution showed that things were more desperate for some than others. I had no wish to lose my fingers, so for now these clothes would have to do. I decided to clean myself up as best I could before proceeding. If the wizard were to find me, I would meet him with a clean face.

I asked directions to the town fountain, happily finding that I could speak the language of these people fluently (though it was not the language of my thoughts). At its mention the gentleman's face lit up.

"Oh, the fountain! Sir, the fountain is the pride of our humble town! You will find it about five hundred paces away, taking a right, a left, and then a right again. Don't forget to say your digoot!"

I nodded knowledgably, and headed in the indicated direction. Five hundred and fifty three paces brought me to the fountain. It stood in one corner of a small square formed by the backs of some impressively large buildings. On the square's edges shop girls gathered in small packs to discuss the latest news from Hadriana while chewing on nabku leaves. A few cast wary glances at me, as if expecting to be called back to duty before they were done.

I approached the fountain, which was indeed quite splendid. As tall as two men, and the water spouted as high as four, falling into a pool with the diameter of two pretty girls lying head to head.

I reached my hands to the water, and closed my eyes, ready for a refreshing splash. But I felt a grip upon my wrists; they were held firm. I opened my eyes, expecting to find myself apprehended by guards or the wizard's men, or subject to a final rally of the words that still bothered me, but no.

The water had risen from the fountain to lock itself around my hands. I looked around, but so far everyone seemed ignorant of this event. I was not the only one at the fountain's edge, and others dipped and splashed gaily without impediment. What had the man said to me? Don't forget your...? I couldn't remember, and even if I had recalled the word I had no idea of its meaning. I watched newcomers approach, but if I had missed some ceremony I could not discern it in their actions.

I looked back to my hands, and then to the water in the fountain. It swirled strangely, then seemed to resolve itself into a word: YOU.

Instantly the grip on my hands was gone, and I

proceeded to wash my hands, face and so far as possible my clothes (I wiped them down with a wet hand) while thinking on this new development. Why had the fountain said YOU to me?

I decided to ask for help.

"I am an honoured visitor to this land," I said to a giggling girl with a stalk dangling from her lip. Her two friends out-did her for giggles. "What can you tell me of the fountain?" It sounded strange to hear a foreign language come from my lips; I trusted I had been a competent speaker of it, otherwise I might find myself getting into trouble with these girls.

She shrugged. "It's a fountain." Her friends laughed.

"No, I mean, is there anything special about it?" I kept my tone polite, my eyes gentle. Was I good-looking? I had yet to see my own face, but I felt that I was, and the eagerness of these girls to talk to me (however unhelpfully) suggested that I was.

The leaf fell from her mouth. "Stop right there, sir traveller! Did the fountain dryad speak to you?"

It was my turn to shrug.

"Oh my god!" they shouted in unison.

The other girls now felt they could chip in. "Don't tell anyone!" the shorter of the three said. "You'll never hear the end of it. They'll have you up before his Lordship, you know!"

"I promise," I said with total sincerity. "I would have said nothing even to you three had I not known from your countenances how trustworthy and thoughtful you were."

"Flatterer!" said the tallest of the three, but she smiled in a way that encouraged me to repeat the offence.

"What does it mean?" I asked.

"There's supposed to be a dryad who lives in the water of the fountain – it was built above an underground lake in which she lives, but upon occasion she surfaces to talk to lucky mortals."

"She only chooses the handsomest," said the shorter girl.

"And the bravest," said the taller girl.

"Then I can only assume her communication was meant for another, and intercepted by yours truly in error."

They all laughed at my modesty, which was nice. I guess I was quite good-looking after all.

"What did she say to you?" asked the first (slightly prettiest) girl.

"You."

"Ooh," said the girls together.

"That means it's a message about you," said the tallest.

"I gathered that much," I said with a smile. "But what does it mean?"

"You won't know till you get the rest of the message, silly," said the shorter one. "She only says one word a day. You'll have to come back to see us every day till you've got the whole thing."

Inwardly I groaned, but outwardly I smiled and said, "I can think of no better fate for a man."

So that was that. The message was obviously going to be an important one, so I decided to wait for it. I had nothing better to do, at least until my memory recovered. And if I should run into my wizardly nemesis during that time I would take the opportunity to do him harm.

I spent the next month in that town, and during that time got to know it very well. It was Amberkad, part of one of the most northerly of the southern city states. Hence my captor's apparent generosity: mungans were ten a copper here. I found myself work as a street sweeper, which was ideal for my purposes. I was able to make my way around the town, poking

into every quiet corner without attracting comment.
The pay was low, but that meant nothing when I had
little purpose for it. Two meals a day were enough to
sustain me, and the town provided a stable for its
employees to kip at night. The generally warm weather
meant few nights were uncomfortable, and once in a
while I let myself be persuaded into spending a few
midnight hours with one of my friends from the
fountain square, though my new employment had
taken some of the shine off my mystery and good
looks. They were still happy to dally with me, but by
the end of the month had mostly ceased to dilly.

What mattered was that the message was coming to
me, word by word. Each morning I would head to the
fountain, wait for the water to grab my hands, and add
one more to the pile. By the end of the month it was
complete, and I resigned my position and prepared
myself for the next stage in the adventure that my life
had become.

"You must find the source of my water and save me
from destruction," said the dryad, very slowly. At that
point I was all set to go and sort things out, if possible,
but I waited till the next day in case there should be
more to the message, and of course there was. "There
will be a reward."

And with that eighteenth word the month of Yessle
was up and I began to collect supplies for a mountain
hike. My shop friends did their best to help, providing
me with scuffed and slightly imperfect goods in return
for promises of continued affection and return visits.
Though I had to some extent lost my appeal for them,
each remained convinced that the dryad's quest would
leave me wealthy and powerful, and none wished to be
the one to miss out. It was the custom in those parts to
take two wives, you see, as it was the custom for a wife
to take two husbands. The system worked at maximum
efficiency when a pair of men and a pair of women all

married each other, but other arrangements were not unknown, and I think all three girls hoped that I would marry them while leaving them free to also select a local husband (each had a sweetheart who would occasionally, accidentally and somewhat hurtfully, I felt, be mentioned in my presence).

In a matter of days I had a selection of warm clothes, a backpack full of supplies, and a short, many-dented sword which had been bought with the savings from my work on the streets. I had discovered nothing more of the wizard, and my subtle attempts to bring up his name provoked no recognition on the part of the girls or my fellow town workers. If he was a resident of this town he kept himself to himself.

I set off for the mountain, killed the demon and then received my reward!

---

3. Three Days in Purple

I had been crowned the king of Amberkad – what a treat! The town had never previously had a king to call its own, and was thrilled at the prospect, especially my three friends from the square. I explained to them that I was not in the right frame of mind for marriage, and they seemed to understand, especially when I presented them with a selection of jewels I'd recovered from the dryad's cave. Effectively that meant they got the benefit of marrying me for which they had hoped without the inconvenience of being my wife. They went away happy after showering me with kisses.

From where did they go away, you ask? For of course Amberkad, never having had a king, did not have a palace. I had been installed in the guest room of the town's lord, something that had been his idea, pressed with the same urgency that he explained the importance of a prime minister to the successful running of the town. I needed no persuasion on either score, and so I spent the first of my days in purple at his house.

The kingly robes with which I had been provided by the grateful dryad were remarkable in their resistance to removal. I tried to take them off to sleep on that first night, but, unsuccessful, I put it down to the remnants of the wizard's spell and lay down to sleep regardless.

In the morning I woke and was glad to see the clothes unruffled themselves when I sat up. There was magic at work, it seemed, but with luck this time it was not inimical. Whoever I had been, it seemed I had a tendency to attract this kind of attention.

There was a knock at the door of my room. "Enter," I called.

"Your Highness," said my new best friend, doffing his hat as he opened the door and came in. "We have a busy day ahead." He was by no means obsequious or fawning; on the contrary, he was simply a good, capable man who wanted me to know what a good, capable man he was.

"Do I have duties already?" I asked, rather surprised. "Don't they normally result from centuries of tradition? Has there been time for them to spring up already?"

"Not quite, your highness," he sat on my bed in a way that I thought was not quite as respectful as it might have been – how horribly quickly I had grown to expect to be treated like a king! I am ashamed of myself retrospectively. "First you have to join us for a breakfast fit for a king. And then you must meet the Queen of Baldir, who has popped over to meet her new peer."

"That was quick!" I said with surprise.

"Royalty is scarcer in the south than in the north, so she is keen to meet a potential mate."

"Mate?"

He laughed at my reaction. "Are you not keen to propagate?"

I shook my head. "I do not even know who I truly am, my new friend. This is a secret I entrust to you because I trust you and your pleasant open face."

He laughed again. "No need to be rude."

I shook my head. "It's true, I do have a measure of amnesia, and though it's slowly coming back to me, I could be anyone or anything."

"That doesn't matter," he said. "You're now the king. Whatever you are, that is what the king should be. Whatever your children are, that is what they should be. It's all decided by the dryad."

"Okay, let's have breakfast first, and talk about the queen later. But first, a clue: is she an attractive woman?"

He looked at me oddly. "Did I say she was a woman?"

I narrowed my eyes and he laughed uproariously.

Breakfast was indeed fit for a king, and after a month of eating minimally it came as a great relief to have such a feast. I stuffed myself on slices of roast harnak, truffled for fried mushrooms, and gorged on chocolate-coated bananas. I washed it down with a flagon of hot tea and blessed the mysterious stars that led me to that place.

As the plates were taken away I let out a mighty burp and asked my prime minister to tell me all about the queen.

"Your highness," he said with a smile, "some surprises are best kept for a particular moment."

The queen was a unicorn!

She trotted up to the castle with a swing in her hips and a flick of her mane. I had to admit, she was a fine filly.

"Hello, your highness," I said with all the charm I could muster.

"King," she said. "I must confess a certain embarrassment; I do not know your name."

"Your embarrassment is shared, and thus halved," I pointed out, "since nor do I."

"A man of mystery?" She kicked at the ground with a hoof.

"Unfortunately," said I.

Wondering what to do next, I decided to show her the fountain from which had sprung my good fortune. "Let me take you to the dryad's fountain," I said, in an unconscious movement placing my hand upon her mane.

"Sir!" It was the prime minister, who did his best to remove my arm without touching my royal person; naturally the attempt was ineffective. "Protocol..!"

I removed my hand in horror. I had stroked the queen's neck. "My profound apologies," I said with a bow that matched my apologies in its profundity.

She whinnied and shook her stately head. "No apologies necessary, dear King. It feels good to be stroked. It's been a long time."

For the rest of the day we were inseparable, and by early evening she had invited me up onto her back for a ride into the woods. As we galloped between the trees in a manner that hardly befitted our royal significances I laid my head upon her soft, warm neck and listened to the pounding of her magnificent heart. Maybe she wasn't a woman, but what a female! We dodged from side to side, and every time I thought I would fall she shifted her body mass to keep me in place. After a period of this I realised the ulterior purpose of these shifts, and gave myself over to pleasure.

As dusk fell, we sat by a stream and talked of love. Each of us saw something in the other that we could not find elsewhere. She saw in me a fellow monarch, one unblinkered by preconceptions and unfettered by convention. I saw in her a lust for life and a joy in movement.

"Are we to be married, then?" I asked.

She shook her head sadly, and nuzzled my neck (being careful to keep her horn well out of the way). "I'm afraid not, my darling."

I turned to her in shock. "But what we're feeling now, that's real, isn't it?"

She licked my ear. "Of course it is, dear King, of course it is."

"Then what's the problem? I realise there's a certain... physical incompatibility. Is that the problem? I'm sure I could find a way to make you happy. We could work it out."

"That's not it, my dear," she said kindly. "It's just that this is the second of your three days in purple. Tomorrow will be your last."

I pressed her for more details, but she refused to say more. Unicorns are magical beings, after a fashion, and have a sense about certain things – or at least that's how I understand it. Was I to die? Or lose my kingship? She would not say, but our love was doomed.

I tried to make the best of it, but the evening was spoilt and we returned to Amberkad in silence.

She dropped me off at the prime minister's house, and I turned to say goodbye.

"We'll see each other tomorrow," she said sadly, pre-empting an awkward farewell.

"I suppose we will."

She pointed at the words that still circled my head. "I'm afraid I can't do anything about those."

I looked up in surprise. "So it's not just me; they're real?"

She tried to nick them with her horn, but words like

"forget" and "amnesia" twisted away like cheeky children. "They should fade with time."

I thanked her and went to my room.

My third day in purple began in much the same way as the second. Once more the robes unruffled themselves when I rose, once more the prime minister knocked on the door, once more I asked him to enter. But this time there was no friendly banter, just an exchange of sad stares. We went downstairs for breakfast, where unfortunately the prime minister's wife decided to bring up the worst possible topic of conversation.

"Yes, Mrs Prime Minister," I replied, "it is a shame that things didn't work out between me and the Queen. You are quite right that it would have been a most unusual union. And you are also right that it would have been good for both our kingdoms. But it was not to be. We had one day of passion and that day was yesterday. Today those of us with futures must look to them, while those without futures must enjoy what time remains."

She sighed sadly and poured me an extra flagon of tea.

I went out to have a look around, pretending to be unconcerned, but it was clear to all around that I was looking for her.

"She's gone, your highness," said the prime minister. "She left in the night, riding away without her retinue. They will follow her today."

I nodded sadly.

"You're not the only one with a broken heart, my lord."

I spent the day as king, and at dusk the robes consumed me.

4. Salacious Grub

I woke up on a hill, my face turned toward the sun. I think that was what had woken me, the sun shining upon my face, charring my eyelids ever so slightly. I sat up and looked around. I had not expected to wake up, so wherever I was, I was happy to be there. I smiled.

Far to the north I could see Amberkad, to the south the town of Brikern. To the west there were two hills. To the east there was a gargantuan grub.

I got to my feet to see it from a different perspective. Surely it could not be *that* big? But it was.

Was this the price of kingship? My final duty as king? I thought not – this was a new day, and the queen had told me that I would have just three days in purple.

I had nothing else planned for the day, so I began to stroll in the direction of the grub. Coincidentally, the grub was moving in the direction of me. This brought us together, at which point I realised the grub was being led on a leash by a tiny man. He stood beside my knee and looked up at me. In turn I looked up at the grub.

"Where are your clothes?" said the man.

I looked down at myself. "Oh, sorry. I hadn't realised. I didn't mean any offence."

"No offence. I was just curious."

"My clothes swallowed me, and then I found myself here."

He shrugged. "These things happen."

"Do they?" I asked. "Do they really?"

He shrugged again. "They do around here."

I nodded. "So I find, if I am honest. Still, it is irksome."

"I can see you are irked." He pointed at his grub. "My

friend David is taking an interest in your nakedness. It is possible that you remind him of a lady grub. I recommend clothing yourself as soon as possible."

I looked up at the salacious grub. "How can you tell?"

"David twitches."

"I see." I looked around me. The landscape was unsurprisingly bare of vestments. "Do you have any suggestions?"

He looked up at David once more and shrugged. "I would suggest running for the nearest town as quickly as you can. He just twitched again."

I paused for breath and began to run to the south. David let out a seeping groan and began to crawl after me.

"Keep running!" called the little man. "You should be alright as long as you keep going. He is persistent but slow."

I waved my thanks without turning and showed him my heels.

This would not be easy: those heels were unshod, and though the ground was grassy it was uneven and dotted with stones. I tried to ignore the pain and run harder, but it was a tactic that could not succeed; the rate at which my feet were being hurt exceeded the rate at which the town approached. Indeed it had barely shifted from the horizon, recalcitrant as a tortoise in its shell. I silently begged it to poke a nose in my direction, but the only thing poking in my direction was the probing, twisting nose of the grub. Surely it knew that it could not mate until it reached maturity? Perhaps it thought we might form a life bond, even at this young age. It could not end well; even a measure of frottage with David would do for me.

What to do then? As I ran I cast my eyes about over and over, like the hook of a fishing rod thrown into a stale pond. Nothing of use presented it to me, and then I noticed a small green object, half-buried in the mud. A broken jug, probably, but if I was lucky a shield, something to hide behind. I put all my energy into a burst of additional speed, hoping to put enough space between David and me to let me dig it up. My fingers drove into the mud, wriggling around the edges of it, pleading with it to rise. Behind me was the hurgling and nurgling of the excited grub, growing ever closer. Even as I felt a spurt of hot fluid upon my shoulders from the anticipating larva, the object came free; it was a mirror, the size of a large plate!

I tucked it under my arm and sprinted off while trying to think of a way to put the mirror to the service of my continued chastity (vis-à-vis grubs, that is).

I had to think of something soon. My feet were threatening to kill me, while the grub was not slackening in its determination. The town was as far away as ever – not literally, but in terms of perspective, at least, as my estimate of the time it would take to reach it rose ever higher.

A mirror. I could use it to reflect the sun, perhaps, into its eyes. Did it have eyes? Or was it hunting me by smell? Could I reflect the sun into its nose, burn it out so I could escape? It seemed unlikely. If I showed the beast its own reflection, would that frighten it away? Unlikely, but it was something I could try in a pinch. If I couldn't escape, perhaps I could attack. If I broke the mirror the pieces of glass could be used as a sword! But a problem: with no means of creating a makeshift handle they would slice my hand as readily as the grub's skin.

My feet left a trail of blood, my body weakened, but my resolve strengthened. I would survive, I would! I refused to die without knowing who I was! I would not die a nobody!

Unfortunately the words of forgetting continued to

revolve about my brow, so the only way to make good on my decision was to defeat my foe!

A thought: who was that foe? How did I really know that the grub was after me? I had only the word of the little man for it. Looking back over my shoulder, I saw that he ran alongside the grub, still holding on to the lead. He was quite definitely smiling.

Hmm.

Why was this man out walking with a grub in the first place? What purpose did he have? In the circumstances, was it unreasonable to wonder if their purpose was to hunt me? Perhaps the grub's lust was real, but harnessed to the little man's foul desires.

The situation was bad; what was to be lost by taking unexpectedly violent action? Nothing. And so I spun on my heel, hefted the mirror, and ran directly at my pursuers. The little man tried to halt the grub in its tracks (one sign at least to confirm my hypothesis) but it could hardly stop so quickly as that; inertia was not its friend. As I ran past the two I slapped the astonished little man on the head with the back of the mirror and grabbed him at the jacket with both hands while the mirror fell to the ground.

As I dashed away, the little fellow slung over my shoulder, the grub began to nose around. Soon it would catch my scent, or see my trail, whatever it is that grubs do, but by then I hoped I would be safe.

From the distance came a shout of "No fair!" followed by one of "All bets are final!" to which a number of incoherent yells replied with anger.

I ignored them, set down my unconscious captive and stripped him of his clothes, up to and including his undergarments. They were of course too small for a relatively big fellow like me, but the trousers stretched far enough to serve me as shorts, and ripping his shirt at the sides allowed me to wear it as a kind of oversized neck tie, covering at least the upper part of my chest. His undergarments – my reluctance being dismissed in an instant by the slow but steady approach of the grub – I wore over each of my arms.

Thus attired, I slapped the fellow to wake him up – he should have at least the opportunity that he had given me – and set off at tender speed in the direction of the voices I had heard.

I had but recently been a king! He who had the temerity to bet against my majestical self would soon learn the error of their ways. I took care to pick up my deadly mirror along the way, in case physical chastisement would be required.

A little over the hill and I was among them – a gaggle of dandies in full frippery. Most were gesticulating with manicured fingers at a ruffian in a rakish hat, though a few off to one side were smiling at each other with the smugness of victory.

I had taken them by surprise; most of the people upon whom they betted must have run quickly in the opposite direction (or perhaps there had never been a survivor before). They were surprised to find me in their midst, more surprised still to find me laying about them with my mirror. I thanked my favourite deity for its preservation and continued solidity with every blow, but after six or seven or eight fellows had fallen to the floor it gave up its life. I held onto a chunk of wood and went for the ruffian, obviously the man responsible for creating my situation. He looked up in alarm and made to say something, but he knew nothing I wished to learn, so I dealt him three sharp blows about the head and kicked him once he hit the floor.

I looked at the dandies, who were looking pointedly at each other's scabbarded fencing swords, though none made a move for his own. I did not recognise any of them, but the fashion of their clothes reminded me of my former kingdom.

"Which of you would like to share his clothes and money with a penniless stranger?" I asked.

Each tried to outpace the other in throwing gold pieces my way, lest he be the one required to give up his finery, but those who had lost out to my victory had least to give, and soon all eyes fell upon a fellow my height who was one of the first to exhaust his financial reserves. I thanked him for his clothes, thanked them all for their money, and prepared to head for Dunnd. There was nothing left for me back in Amberkad; I knew that the wizard was not there, nor anyone who could restore my memory. I would press on to a new town, to new adventures, to new opportunities. As I crested the hill once again I saw my friend the little man, running in the same direction in which I was now walking. I caught him up and returned his clothes, which he put on gratefully, and we walked at our ease away from the grub, which now ambled aimlessly.

"Sorry about the bang on the head," I said somewhat gruffly.

"I understand," he said. "And I apologise for hunting you with the grub, and the initial deception necessitated by my employment in that regard."

"I understand," I said in my turn. "One has to make a living."

"In that regard, sir, I am now somewhat inconvenienced. By any chance would you be needing a man-at-arms, butler, assistant, squire or anything in that regard? I note that you are now well-equipped as regards gold pieces."

"I am indeed, and I suppose in a way I have you to thank for that, little man. Come then, join me."

"Thank you, sir," he said happily. "My name is Dannoil. And your name, sir?"

"If only I knew, Dannoil. If only I knew."

The Riches

Tim Jeffreys

Alone on a hillside high above the sleeping city sat Peter, fingers before a small fire. He had been travelling for a month on foot. He had travelled by day and – sometimes – by night, and had seen all kinds of wonders along the way. Now he merely sat and waited. He waited and waited, staring into the night. At last he got up and asked of the darkness:

"I've travelled a long way and there is no one here to meet me. Have I arrived too late?"

At his voice there was a rustle in the nearby bushes and a shape emerged out of the night. Peter stared as a little blue man, the devil Rowernac, moved forward into the light of the flames. And the little blue devil said, "No, Peter! You are just in time!"

"Now, wait!" a voice called out of the darkness. There was the sound of quick footsteps approaching and someone's laboured breathing, before another man appeared out of the night. He walked with a pained step. His hair had been allowed to grow long over the collar of his jacket and his face had a month's growth of beard. His eyes were wild, his face hard and fixed in concentration. Seeing Rowernac sat by the fire with Peter his expression turned accusatory.

"Just wait," he said. "I'm here. Just wait."

"Ah, Louis," said the devil with a playful smirk. "You have arrived."

"But... Peter got here first?" Louis said, turning his

expression on the other man. "That's impossible. He must have cheated."

"There was no cheating," Rowernac said in a calm voice. "I would not have allowed it."

"Then how could he have possibly got here before me? I walked all day every day and through most of the nights, hardly pausing to eat or sleep. Look at me, I'm exhausted. And look at him sitting there, shaved and fed and happy as Larry."

"Larry?" said the devil, pondering a moment. "Louis, I think you misunderstood the rules of the challenge I set you both. I never said it was a race."

It was exactly one month ago to the day when Peter and Louis, long-time friends and explorers both, had happened upon Rowernac's lair whilst mapping caves beneath the hills where they now stood. The cavern was piled high with gold and jewels, more riches than either man had ever dared to imagine. The little blue devil, lolling amongst this splendour with a smirk on his face, looked up in delight at the two men who had invaded his sanctum.

"I am the devil Rowernac and this is my home. Trespassing here is punishable by death!"

The two men swallowed and glanced at each other. They began to inch backwards.

"Stop!" said Rowernac. "There's no escape. All I have to do is wave my hand and the ceiling of the tunnel behind you will cave in and bury you both alive!"

He glared at them, his dark eyes full of mischief and glee, and opening his mouth he ran his tongue over a set of fierce-looking fangs.

"What will you do to us?" Peter asked.

"You're not going to... eat us, are you?" asked Louis.

Rowernac grinned and considered a moment.

"I might. I might eat you."

"No!"

"Or I might peel off your skins and turn them into a blanket for my bed."

"What? No! Not that!"

"Or cut off your heads and use them for a foot rest."

"God help us!"

"Or!" he said, leaping up.

"Or what? Tell us! Tell us!"

"Or..." Rowernac looked from one man to the other for a long moment, considering each in turn.

"What? What?"

"Or maybe I will challenge you instead."

"What?" said the confounded men in unison. Then: "Yes! That! That! A challenge!"

"Very well. What about this. I will send you both on a journey. One to one corner of the land, one to another. You will travel separately and be here back at this hill in exactly one month's time. When you get here one of you will have untold riches. For the other it will be a punishment."

The two men looked at each other.

"Well, I suppose that's better than being eaten."

"Much better!" said the devil. The two men looked beyond him, their gaze shifting about the piled treasures. "I remind you – one will be given unimaginable riches. The other a punishment. Are you ready to begin?"

"Yes," said Peter.

"Yes," said Louis.

Then, before anything more could be said, Rowernac snapped his fingers and the two vanished from his lair. He had transported them by magic far across the land, one to one corner, one to another just as he had threatened. After some initial bewilderment, both realised what had happened and, recalling the promised riches, began at once to make their way back to that hill, using all the tools and knowledge and exploring experience they had at their disposal.

A month is a long time on the road. Louis, thinking back to when he and Peter first chanced upon Rowernac in his lair, could not quite remember the exact details of the agreement.

"You said the first one back would be given riches!" he said.

"No," said the devil. "That was not what I said at all. Now then, Louis, tell me about your journey."

"My journey? What is there to tell? There were fields and rivers and cities to cross. I was cold and sodden and hungry most of the time. I was worn out by the road. The rain drenched me. The sun burned me. There were ugly mountains in the way. I walked and walked. And there were always people trying to slow me down. I ignored them of course. When I needed food I stole it from their market stalls. I drank riverwater. I was thinking all the time about those riches you promised, I focused my mind on them, and now that I get here it seems that Peter will get them instead as he arrived first."

Peter spoke up. "It's true it makes no sense that I arrived before you, Louis, as I must admit I lingered along the way. I watched the stars. I couldn't help myself. I sat and stared at clouds. I swam in wild lakes. It was all so beautiful. The sun was warm, and the rain washed me. And there were people I met and some of them walked with and we talked to pass the time away. Some of them took me in and gave me food and a bed for the night, sometimes out of kindness and sometimes in exchange for a day's work. In one town I met a young woman as golden as the summer and I lay with her in a field until sunset. And what a sunset! What colours! And the sunrises, and the nights sleeping under oak trees, with only the sound of the wind and nothing else. And those stars above. So many stars. What a world there is out there! What a world! What a journey!"

When Peter finished talking, Louis turned from him to Rowernac, his eyes alight with anger.

"You sent me further away than him! He had a shorter journey! He must have! How else could he have had all this time for women and sunsets!"

"It was never a question of distance, Louis," Rowernac said.

"But that's not fair!"

"Fair or not, you must accept that you have lost."

Louis tried to speak but he was impotent with rage. He saw, though, that the little devil would not be argued with, so gave a deep sigh and said:

"What is it then? What's my punishment?"

"Why," said Rowernac. "Don't you know? You have already had it."

Louis gazed at the devil in bewilderment, his mouth trying to form words.

Peter stood up. The three stood looking at each other in the light of the fire. There was an awkward silence for some minutes until Peter was forced to speak.

"Are you going to give me the riches now?"

"Why, Peter," said Rowernac. "Don't you understand either? I already have."

Peter's face tightened with confusion. He glanced from the devil to Louis, from Louis to the devil. Then his eyes cleared as, all at once, he understood. He nodded and was silent.

"Now take what I have given you and go," Rowernac said. And the two men turned and, glancing back only once at the devil who sat on a rock watching them and laughing, began to walk down the hillside towards the waiting city.

The Quarterly Review

Reviews by
Stephen Theaker,
Jacob Edwards,
Douglas J. Ogurek
and Tim Atkinson

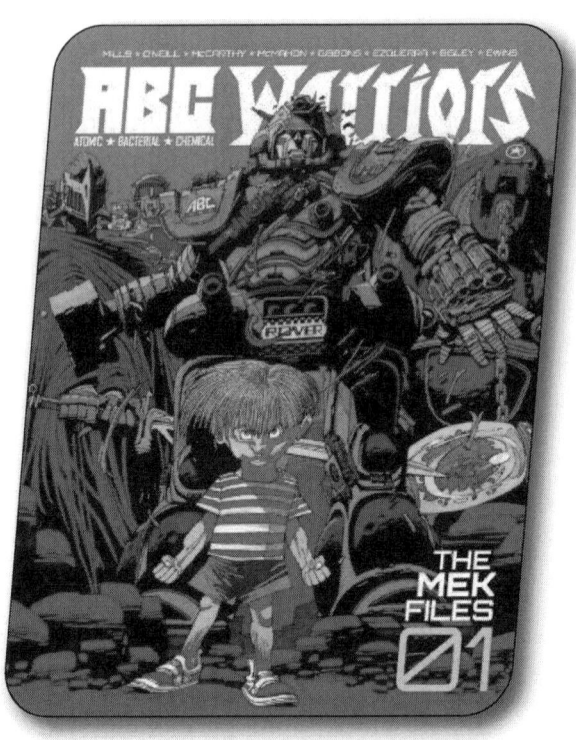

A.B.C. Warriors: The Mek Files 01

Reviewed by Stephen Theaker

The stories in **A.B.C. Warriors: The Mek Files** 01
(Rebellion, tpb, 308pp) are all written by Pat Mills,
with artwork from a superstar cast of artists that
includes Kevin O'Neill (*League of Extraordinary
Gentlemen*), Dave Gibbons (*Watchmen*), Brendan
McCarthy, Mick McMahon, Carlos Ezquerra, Brett
Ewins, and Simon Bisley – the only one I hadn't heard
of before is the mysterious S.M.S. With a line-up like
that you'd expect the book to be much better than it is,
but it's still pretty good.

The first batch of stories, drawn in a relatively straightforward and readable style, date from 2000AD's early days – issues 119 to 139, from 1979. Here we see a group of eccentric robots joining Sergeant Hammer-stein for a special mission: Happy Shrapnel, Joe Pineapples, Deadlock (Grand Wizard of the Knights Martial), immense, vengeful Mongrol, reprogrammed Volgan war criminal General Blackblood, and molten monster The Mess. It's gleefully violent: you wouldn't give it to a child nowadays without asking a parent first. Once the team are assembled, they are packed off to tame Mars, the devil planet! The premise sets them up for a long run, but after dealing with cyboons, mutants, the red death, robot tyrannosaurs, and big George with five brains (none of which work properly), it wraps up very suddenly with a declaration that "we've straightened out this side of Mars now". I enjoyed all of these stories, though they're not so memorable that I didn't realise until later that I'd already read them in the 2002 Titan collection *The Mek-Nificent Seven*.

The strip returned to 2000AD in 1988, nine years and four hundred issues later, the long gap perhaps explained by the problems that had "plagued the strip from beginning to end" (according to Kevin O'Neill, speaking in a reprint volume from 1983): "Group stories are like breaking rocks for writer and artist alike. Pat Mills broke the biggest rocks and the splinters flew off in all directions."

The new setting – the future Earth known as Termight – suggests that in the interval the warriors have been involved in the adventures of Nemesis the Warlock. Joined by Ro-Jaws, Hammer-stein's old friend from the Ro-Busters, and then Terri, a human who thinks of herself as a robot, the team battles foes including The Monad, the quintessence of human evil from the end of the world, who causes havoc after escaping into the time wastes. The art in this half of the book by Simon Bisley and S.M.S. is admirable in many ways – it's challenging, energetic and expressive – but it's difficult to tell what is going on, especially when events take place in one tunnel after another, with backgrounds often entirely white or entirely black. It's trying very hard to be grown up and significant, and though the stories are still being written by Pat Mills, these aren't half as much fun. I would probably pass on volume 02 if it took the same approach.

Though the two parts are so different that it's like reading a book that's half Curt Swan, half recent Frank Miller, I liked it overall. Its best ideas are brilliant – poor old George staggering across the surface of Mars while his hands and feet argue with his head! – and it still comes as a surprise to see robot heroes killing humans, when mainstream entertainment so often goes out of its way to give human heroes zombies or robots to murder. I wouldn't say that appealed, exactly (you'd worry about me if it did), but it felt honest.

Apocalypse Now Now

Reviewed by Tim Atkinson

With fantasy these days increasingly resembling the long tail of YA fiction, it's a post-Potter world in which we're living now.

And **Apocalypse Now Now**, the debut novel by South African Charlie Human, exemplifies that shift. Cannily positioned on the cusp of YA and proper grown-up fantasy, it owes a sizeable debt to J.K.

Rowling's creation, even when it's reacting against it. Indeed, much of its appeal comes from its simultaneous celebration and subversion of the usual teenage wish-fulfilment tropes against the colourful backdrop of Cape Town.

Its schoolboy protagonist, the spectacularly named Baxter Zevcenko, finds himself on a mission to rescue his girlfriend from forces unknown, acquiring plot tokens and magical powers on the way. So far, so Potter.

But his school – a pivotal and vividly described location for the novel's early scenes – is no Hogwarts, reeling from the impact of gang warfare and the aftermath of a pupil's murder. Baxter himself is thriving there, masterminding a porn distribution network with his friends and accomplices.

His Holden Caulfield-style first-person narration is one of *Apocalypse*'s triumphs. Despite his porn business and general air of superiority, Baxter's funny, insightful and crucially, *he's likeable*. He surprises himself as he discovers he's willing to move heaven and earth for the people he cares about.

This is fortunate, because that's exactly what he has to do.

Baxter's school experience prepares him well for the only marginally more dangerous and Darwinian supernatural underworld of Cape Town to which his quest takes him. En route to finding his girlfriend, he meets African legends walking the earth, experiences psychic flashbacks to his Boer ancestors, tangles with occult Government operatives and parasitic spiders, and – as advertised in the title – finds himself staring the end of the world in the face.

Our hero's adult guide through this world, Dr Jackie Ronin, is another of the book's trump cards. An approximate hybrid of John McClane, Catweazle and Dr Gonzo, this special forces veteran and self-proclaimed occult detective is a great foil for Baxter and a confirmed scene-stealer.

Reviewing a first novel is essentially looking for promise – and there's much promise to find in *Apocalypse*. It's cute, fast-paced and offers an appealing mix of old, new, borrowed and blue (movies). And it's always pleasing to encounter a modern-dressed fantasy not mining the exhausted seams of Norse or Greek mythology for inspiration.

But it's not quite the complete package.

Structurally, considerable time is spent in the first few chapters introducing the school, the conflicts within it *and* Baxter's gang of friends, only for all this to be sidelined for much of the kidnapping which starts fifty pages in. It isn't a long book, but even so it feels like two plots – the home front and the quest – have been stitched together in a way that you can still see the joins.

Apocalypse's brevity also exacerbates the sense that Baxter's assumption of his ancestral powers hasn't been properly earned. He doesn't have to work for his magic, and even poster boys for wish fulfilment like our Harry have to do that. The final showdown manages to amplify this power-trip to ridiculous proportions while also being a tonal misstep into Michael Bay-does-giant-robots territory.

These slips, together with some plot contrivances that don't bear too close investigation, bear out a sense that Human lacks full control of his material. Yet the quality of the narration, the novelty of the setting and the subversive homage of the premise combine to make *Apocalypse* a punchy read and an auspicious beginning.

Looking forward to reading the sequel? You bet.

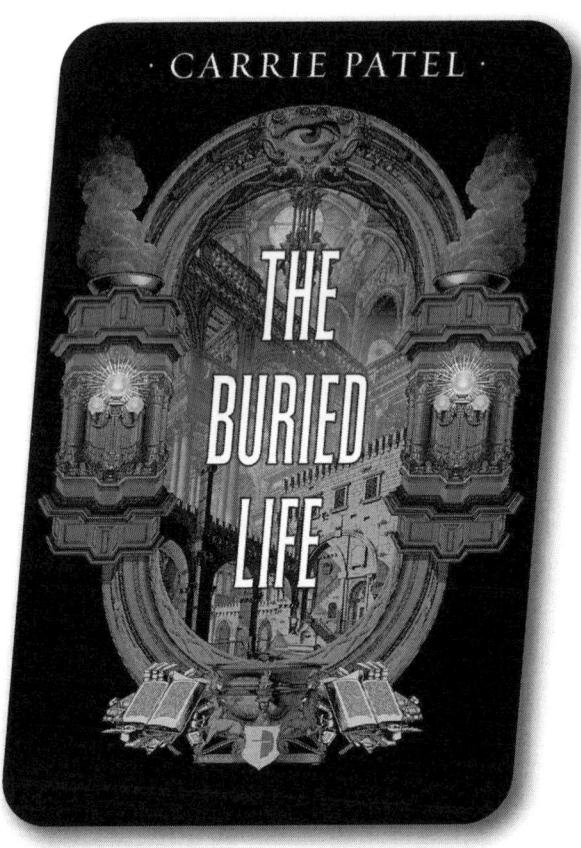

The Buried Life

Reviewed by Stephen Theaker

In **The Buried Life** (Angry Robot, ebook, 4443ll) Carrie Patel tells the story of two women. Jane Lin is a laundry woman trusted by the height of high society to deal with their dirtiest and daintiest unmentionables. Liesl Malone is a police officer, currently getting used to a new partner with a theatrical background. They are brought together by a series of murders: Malone is shut out of the investigation – at least officially – but won't let that stop her getting at the truth, while Jane is knocked unconscious after stumbling across the body of a Mr Fitzhugh during a late night laundry run. A conspiracy is afoot!

Mystery builds. Death will strike again. People scurry in the dark after curfew. Secret pasts abound. Motivations emerge from the shadows. Orphans discover how their parents died &c. Jane stays involved in all this at the prompting of Malone, who has no other way in to this world, but also on account of her own attraction, despite herself, to surly, sexy Roman Arnault, reputedly a button man for the council. He takes a shine to her, and literally sweeps her off her feet at a dance before saying, "I could show you who I am, what I do, and why they run. But will you like what you find?"

Roman is the kind of melodramatic anti-hero that seems to be all over fantasy at the moment, thanks maybe to the commercial success of Cullen and Grey, though of course they're part of a long tradition of literary gits, going back through Mr Darcy and Pamela's Mr B. Whether you find that type appealing may affect your enjoyment of the book. Jane has it bad – "Something in her chest fluttered as she watched him unnoticed" – but he didn't do much for me. By the end he seems rather less significant and interesting than at first, and rather too many mysteries are resolved by him deciding to explain, just because at last he feels like it.

So far you might think this a Victorian novel, and it rather felt like one. However, it is set in the future, hundreds of years after a disaster. Far enough ahead for time to rub away most of the letters on a copper plaque, but close enough that paper books have survived and can still be read. Events take place, for the most part, in the underground city of Recoletta, but these people aren't mutated – physically or psychologically – by the centuries underground. This isn't, say, *The Caves of Steel*: when Malone visits the surface she's awed by the big sky, but not so much that it stops her climbing on the roof of a moving train.

There is nothing like the sense we get in *City of Ember* that keeping an underground city going might be difficult – though we do hear briefly about "orphans and unfortunates ... working twelve-hour shifts on factory machines and assembly lines" – nor is there any shocking reality-shifting revelation upon emergence like the one in *The Hero of Downways*. Recoletta felt to me like Victorian London with a roof, its most unusual feature a ruling class who grow their nails slightly long because they can. The discoveries on the surface will feel old hat even to people who haven't seen *Logan's Run* or read *Kamandi*. It's hard not to groan at the cheesiness of Roman revealing the collected Shakespeare he keeps in a hidden compartment.

For me, a hurdle the book struggled to clear was its initial similarity to *City of Stairs*, which also begins with the murder of an academic but heads off in more appealingly fantastical directions. *The Buried Life* doesn't have any new science fiction ideas to offer, and for the most part it stays stubbornly away from anyone who plays an active role in events. Yet for all that it was an enjoyable enough novel. I had a good time reading it and found most of the characters appealing. I worried about the danger they were in, hoped they would make it out alive, and was sad when some didn't. I probably wouldn't read a sequel, and I don't expect this one to stick with me, but I'd look out for other books from the same author to see if they had a more interesting premise.

The Clockwork Muse

Reviewed by Stephen Theaker

I wish I had read **The Clockwork Muse** (Harvard, pb, 112pp) by Eviatar Zerubavel a decade or so ago. If I had, maybe I'd have an MA from the OU now instead of a measly postgraduate diploma. My dissertation work was interrupted by our first baby – boo-hoo, poor me! – but this would have taught me to plan properly for that interruption, and to keep pushing forward, rather than waiting for an endlessly receding week off when I would catch up on everything.

It is a short but intensely useful book about the importance of scheduling time for writing and making an ongoing effort instead of relying on unpredictable bursts of inspiration. As the title indicates, it's an unromantic view of the creative process. Who would want a clockwork muse, you'd think? But as the subtitle says, this is "A Practical Guide" to getting the book done, a guide to doing the job without leaving blood on the keyboard and a trail of broken marriages in your wake.

Of course, some of my favourite books are by writers who drank all day and wrote all night hopped up on speed, but for most of us that would not be terribly productive. The goal set by this book is "to establish a regular writing routine that would actually work", and the way to do that is by creating "a comfortable fit between your writing and the rest of your life". This is for people who want to finish their books, and finish their books on schedule, saving the drama for the page.

There are similarities to the thinking behind NaNoWriMo: whether writing a thesis, dissertation or a book, *The Clockwork Muse* encourages writers to plan the length of a writing project, identify times you can and can't write, take the pressure off a first draft, write whether you're in the mood or not, and develop the habit of steadily writing. The difference is that NaNoWriMo is a short sprint, shoving aside everything from your life for a single month.

This book aims to help with longer-term projects. It certainly doesn't suggest trying to write a huge amount in one great heave. In fact, Zerubavel explains that he normally plans "to write only a page and a half a day", two or three at most. He explains that "setting a sustainable pace will certainly help increase your chances of meeting your deadlines and avoiding disappointment and failure later on".

When I come to write another novel, I'll be certain to follow the advice given here – for example marking off well in advance the days on the calendar when I already know I won't be able to write, and planning accordingly. Many of you may have to fit your writing in amongst the demands of work and the pleasures of family: get yourself a copy of this book. Even if you have to buy an expensive second-hand copy, it'll pay off in the long term.

Costume Not Included

Reviewed by Stephen Theaker

When last we left him, Chesney Arnstruther had set himself up as a superhero – The Actionary – found himself a nice girlfriend, Melda McCann, and caused significant problems for the bad guys, up to and including Lucifer himself. It was trouble twixt heaven and hell that got him his super-powers in the first place, a by-product of a negotiation between the two post-mortem destinations. That all happened in *The Damned Busters,* book one in the To Hell and Back series, reviewed in #37. **Costume Not Included** (Angry Robot, ebook, 4432ll) is book two, and it continues from the first book pretty much directly.

Chesney's "weasel-headed, sabertooth-fanged" demon Xaphan is now much friendlier, having grown accustomed to the benefits that come with working for the Actionary. Chesney's over-protective mother Letitia has taken up with the Reverend Billy Lee Hardacre, a top-rated television preacher who plans to announce The Actionary as the prophet of a new era. Crime rates are low, thanks to the city's new superhero, and so Chesney ends up investigating a cold case, the disappearance of a journalism student nine years ago, which quickly blows hot.

As with the superheroics of the first book, the most entertaining element of *Costume Not Included* might be considered a spoiler, were it not shown in Tom Gauld's excellent cover illustration. Yes, that's Jesus typing on a laptop at the bottom (or at least one version of him), brought into the story by Chesney to write a new Bible. Hardacre thinks the universe is a book being written by God, and maybe he's right – trouble is, this Jesus comes from an earlier draft. It's amusing to see how the conversation between Jesus and a modern-day television evangelist might go.

If you're a fan of the TV show *Community*, imagine how Abed might cope with almost infinite power in a world of angels and demons and you'll have a good sense of this book. If the Actionary dangled me over the edge of a tall building, I'd say whatever he wanted me to say. If he created a safe environment for me to express my feelings honestly, I'd admit I prefer this writer's far future science fantasy to these modern day superheroics, but I enjoyed this book more than the first, perhaps because all the pieces of the world were in place and the author could just start playing with them.

Edge of Tomorrow

Reviewed by Jacob Edwards

*Henceforth, the deceitful must roll a giant jaffa up
Hollywood Hill.*

    Most of Europe has fallen to an alien invasion.
Humanity faces extinction. And yet, a new high-tech
battle armour brings hope, this being symbolised by
Sergeant Rita Vrataski (Emily Blunt) who, thus kitted
out as a new recruit, was able to kill hundreds of alien
"Mimics" in a single day. On the back of this,

mankind's first victory, the combat gear goes into mass production and the army into recruitment overdrive, massing for a counteroffensive. As Major William Cage (Tom Cruise), glib spokesman for the powers that be, sitting safe at HQ, is pressganged into the front line as insurance against an anticipated public relations backlash post-war, so the scenario is set for **Edge of Tomorrow** (dir. Doug Liman), an action SF film based on Japanese writer Hiroshi Sakurazaka's illustrated novella *All You Need is Kill*. Cage dies within the first few minutes of fighting, doused in the acidic blood of an alien he's managed to take down. Face dissolving, he screams... and regains consciousness the day before battle.

Spoilers, inevitably, but then again the movie's tagline is: LIVE. DIE. REPEAT. So, not too hard to figure out.

Yes, it's *Groundhog Day* rendered as serious SF. (Although with sufficient humour that a homage wouldn't have gone astray – the drill sergeant slapping Cage awake with a call of, "It's Groundhog Day, soldier!", perhaps, in preparation for the D-Day styled landing that's to come.) The Mimics, it transpires, have evolved the ability to manipulate time. Hence, whenever one of their "Alphas" (a rare breed) is killed, the "Omega" (the brain behind it all) rewinds the clock by a day, resetting events but retaining the Alpha's knowledge of what has transpired. This makes the aliens nigh invincible, but it's also their Achilles' heel. Through inadvertently being turned into a quasi-Alpha (as was Vrataski before him), Cage is able to replay the day prior to his first death, learning from his mistakes and so progressing deeper and deeper into the battle scenario. Computer gaming is an obvious motif here, but the repetition is handled quite well, the viewer being to a large extent shielded from the Sisyphean drudgery that occasionally threatens

Cage with despair. Through trial and error all things should eventually be possible, but can Cage and Vrataski find and kill the Omega before Cage himself is hunted down and drained of his new faculties? The scene is set for a SF classic.

Or at least will be, should *Edge of Tomorrow* die at the box office and take some critical comments back to director Doug Liman and company pre-filming. If not then we're stuck with what we see; namely, a wonderful premise that has been artificially bent so as to take the shape of a big fat audience hook.

Love him or hate him, objectively Tom Cruise does a good job in portraying Cage through a gamut of personas. Emily Blunt delivers the perfect mix of prowess and pathos, and may well relegate Sigourney Weaver and Linda Hamilton to lesser places on the SF podium of empowerment. Brendan Gleeson is charismatically cheerless in support; and so, in terms of acting, the money has been well spent. And yet Warner Bros. also invested upwards of $100 million in marketing *Edge of Tomorrow* – retitled from Sakurazaka's original due to perceived public negativity evinced by the word "Kill" – and there seems to have been an unhealthy level of attention given to charting pre-release audience hype and anticipating how strongly the film would open at the box office,[1] rather than simply making the best movie possible and trusting to an appreciation of quality. Advertising posters showed Blunt and Cruise with pride of place given to their battle armour – the spectacle rather than the substance of a production that didn't yet have much, the script itself at this stage still lingering through a process of being reworked, re-authored, revised, then re-authored twice more, yet still having no ending by the time that filming commenced.[2] Whether this is more damning of Liman (who at least was striving for a finale, albeit graspingly) or of Warner Bros. (who clearly didn't care one way or the other), what emerges is an alarming imperative to market first, shoot later and ask questions only in retrospect, all the while making concessions to some profiler's forecast of what today's audience must want, expect and (que será, será) be given. One might suspect that this is not how the SF masterpieces of the past came to be made.

Edge of Tomorrow is engrossing, to be sure, and has fought its way to the silver screen without having had its brains blown out; yet, still it has sacrificed something of its artistic vision in pandering to the bottom line, and the supposed tastes of a first- and second-weekend opening crowd. In Sakurazaka's novella, which is set in Japan, the Mimics take their form from starfish that alien nanobots have forcibly evolved. The beach setting therefore makes sense, but the creatures themselves less so when their initial incursion has been transposed to central Europe. Furthermore, the Mimics are invested with too great a power (oh, blessed effects) to function naturally within a plot that has punched several holes through itself while being many times re-scripted for benefit of Hollywood's unnatural selection. That the aliens are waiting in ambush suggests that humanity's charge through France must have played out at least once before, and with sufficient effectiveness to kill an Alpha. Notwithstanding Cage's first-mission bumbling, however, it is difficult to imagine how this could be the case. Vrataski has lost her pseudo-Alpha abilities (or so she feels; presumably she hasn't tested this), and without her carefully rehearsed revisions, the army must surely have had about as much chance of mounting a successful onslaught as the actors would have if called upon to extemporise all their dialogue in Japanese. Moreover, it is manifestly unclear why the campaign is being fought by ground soldiers. Memories of Iraq? Normandy? Gallipoli? Yes, it's something of a paean to futility and our vivid and confronting history of military blunders, but in this instance there are no civilians to worry about; no technological limitations as per World War Two or One. Therefore... Rockets, anyone? Lots of lovely guided missiles, stockpiled for a rainy day and dusted off at last to blow the shiitake out of something multi-leggèd and squidgy? No? Well, maybe next time.

All told, *Edge of Tomorrow* has too many contrivances – Cage's blinkered lack of initiative; Dr Carter's magic Omega-locator; whatever banal version of the ending is showing today – to qualify for anything more celebrated than a single viewing; which is a shame, because for much of that viewing it presents as a film that might not be out of place on the hallowed DVD shelf of SF for the ages. In the end, though, this was Hollywood trying to convince itself while publicity ringmasters inculcated upon prospective audiences the importance of forming sale day queues outside the cinema. History will show that *Edge of Tomorrow*, sharp-toothed specimen though it may be, was sharp in the wrong places, over-evolved to meet the glittery requirements of Tinseltown's creative cul-de-sac. Gloss up. Dumb down. Market. Repeat. Thus runs the tepid loop, Alpha blockbusters reporting back to executive Omegas while viewers wait helpless and unknowing for tomorrow to come.

---

1. Cheney, Alexandra, "Warner Bros., Tom Cruise Gear Up to Make Sure 'Tomorrow' Never Dies", variety.com, May 19, 2014 [https://variety.com/2014/film/news/warner-bros-tom-cruise-gear-up-to-make-sure-tomorrow-never-dies-1201183917/]
2. Lee, Chris, "Doug Liman hopes his wild loop means a hit with 'Edge of Tomorrow'", latimes.com, May 31, 2014 [http://www.latimes.com/entertainment/movies/la-et-mn-ca-doug-liman-20140601–story.html#page=1]

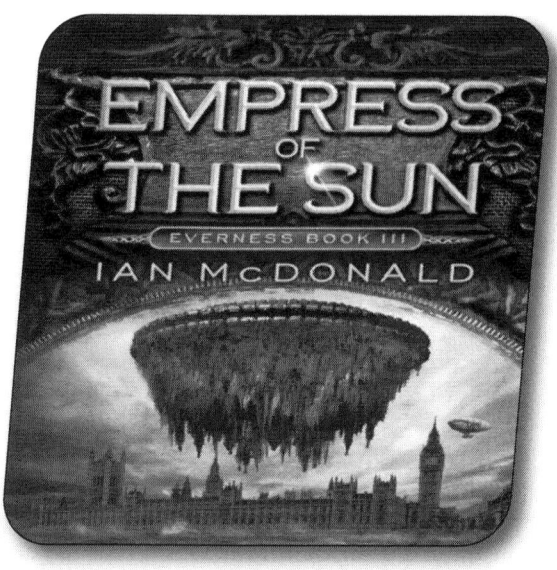

Empress of the Sun

Reviewed by Stephen Theaker

Ian McDonald's **Empress of the Sun** (digital audiobook, Audible, 10 hrs 40 mins), read by Tom Lawrence, is on the whole a audiobook of two sides. One deals with Everett Singh, off on an airship, *Everness*, that can slide between alternative Earths with a rough and ready crew. In this adventure they find themselves on an Earth where the dinosaurs never died out, and their evolution and development continued, to the point where they were powerful enough to re-engineer most of the solar system into a great torus around the sun.

The other side of the book concerns the alternative-world Everett who has taken his place back home, and his efforts to avoid detection. That's not the kind of thing his cyborg powers make any easier, especially when you add best friends and potential girlfriends to the mix – it's hard to resist showing off. He is originally from a world ruled by beings who powered him up and sent him off to make trouble elsewhere, and they aren't too happy that he has gone off-mission.

A lot of the book's fun comes from the efforts of the two boys to interact with members of the opposite sex: bolshy captain's daughter Sen on one side, snarky schoolgirl Noomi on the other. One girl shows her interest by making crude comments on the ship's deck, the other starts a Facebook page devoted to the cyborg's bum, asking people to vote on snapshots taken while he's keeping goal. All the awkwardness should resonate with a teenage readership, and at least amuse older readers.

The reading by Tom Lawrence is good, the characters easy to tell apart, the narration moving from action to comedy to drama without ever running into trouble. I wouldn't be in a hurry to listen to or read earlier or later books in the series, of which this is the third instalment – it's aimed at a younger audience than me, and it doesn't push my particular buttons. But I don't begrudge the time I spent listening to it, and I finished the whole thing over the course of two or three days, pretty much the fastest I've ever listened to a full-length audiobook novel.

Ernest et Célestine
(aka Ernest & Celestine)

Reviewed by Jacob Edwards

A one-bear band and a winter's dream for two.

Ernest et Célestine is the story of a bear and a mouse, who through the shared bond of imagination and creativity forge the most unlikely of friendships at odds with the proscriptive bigotry of their aboveground and belowground societies. Ernest is a musician, hungry and busking; Célestine an artist, orphaned and reluctantly indentured to the clinic of tooth collection and restoration. When Célestine dissuades Ernest from eating her, and instead leads him to the storeroom of a lolly shop, the sweet-toothed bear and the dreamy mouse end up on the run from their respective police. These implacable forces – lawful and righteous upholders of the great prejudice – in one poignantly damning scene find themselves to have accidentally mingled while in pursuit, and must each beat a wary retreat. They are suspiciously alike in their antipathy towards the two fugitives, just as Ernest and Célestine are alike in repudiating the conventional wisdom. It is a simple parable, guilelessly enacted.

Ernest et Célestine is an animated film, but not of the computer-modelled, hyper-realistic school from which we see graduate a larger, slicker cohort every year. Whereas its American counterparts revel in the new technologies and give us fully malleable, three-dimensional animations and a myriad of camera shots to show off each permutation, *Ernest et Célestine* evokes the old school, hand-drawn approach and for the most part is filmed in wide shot, as if we're looking at a picture book. Instead of jump cuts and close-ups and micro-focus on detail, each scene plays out broadly and *in toto*, classic and quaint, as if running frame-to-frame along the fast-thumbed, flickering edge of a sketchbook. Nostalgia aside, this is somehow very engaging; and of course, the faster the characters move, the more chaotic the spectacle. The style is well suited both to heartfelt quiet moments and to the frenetic galumphing of bears in enclosed spaces.

Based on the eponymous series of books by Belgian author-illustrator Gabrielle Vincent (penname of Monique Martin), *Ernest et Célestine* is, by and large, a warm family hug of a tale, and one that would retain much of its cosy sensibility even if watched undubbed or without subtitles. There are some dark overtones, however, to the bear and mice societies, where utopian conformity is never far removed from browbeating and the heavy truncheon of a police state. The topside bears are fearful of the mice, who serve as *de facto* tooth fairies and so underpin the bear cubs' formative introduction to consumerism. The mice, meanwhile, think very highly of the well-ordered commune they've nibbled out of the sewers, yet are incisor-obsessed and vilifying of the bears, and thus have become zealously concerned with maintaining their own insular existence. Capitalist enterprise versus communist dogma? Perhaps. And though the overall tone of *Ernest et Célestine* is that of a children's picture book, individual characters are shaded in accordance with the strength of their misconvictions, the resulting grotesquery on occasion calling to mind the deformed cartoons that Gerald Scarfe produced for *Pink Floyd – The Wall*. Amidst the soft watercolours established by Gabrielle Vincent for her fantasy realm, the happily ever after never seems too far away, but nor entirely does the frightening dystopia that lurks beneath Ernest's and Célestine's nightmares and within the writhing, demonic surge of the mouse police.

Vincent is said by director Benjamin Renner to have upheld a childlike ingenuousness in her art, keeping the scariness of the world at bay by immersing herself in its charms.[1] Renner and co-directors Vincent Patar and Stéphane Aubier evidently have sketched their film designs from this outlook, and in doing so have brought *Ernest et Célestine* to life as a touching and innocent yet menacing at the edges winter fable: a fitting tribute indeed to a greatly beloved author and her two most famous creations. Those viewers who lay claim to an especially nuanced ear might detect actor Lambert Wilson – who played The Merovingian in *The Matrix Reloaded* and *The Matrix Revolutions* – voicing

Ernest in the original, French language release of
Ernest et Célestine, while those who have attained
complete mastery of the apperceptive arts will also
distinguish Lauren Bacall as the doom and gloom
orphanage caretaker in the English dub. This latter
piece of casting seems particularly fitting, given that
Bacall (born 1924) and Vincent (1928–2000) were
contemporaries, and that Bacall – unlike the gavel-
wielding bears and mice who so fervidly seek to
condemn Ernest and Célestine – has long been a
proponent of liberal democracy. *Ernest et Célestine* is
both sentimental and gently didactic, but it is also very
funny; and this ubiquitous humour, rather than being
pitched at viewers of different ages and then
shoehorned into the script where specially signposted,
blossoms instead with spontaneity, and springs up
throughout as a natural and heartily observed
corollary of the story. Making no obvious distinction
between adults and children, yet remaining equally
appealing to both, *Ernest et Célestine* is a lovely film
that in years to come may well garner unto itself that
much-coveted and (in this instance) tenderly
bestowed accolade: timeless.

Directed by Stéphane Aubier, Vincent Patar, and Benjamin
Renner, released 12 December 2012 (French, with subtitles);
28 February 2014 (English dub).

---

1.   Benjamin Renner, "*Ernest et Célestine* Making Of', Blog
      25, posted 19 March 2014
      [http://ernestandcelestine.tumblr.com/post/8007342221
      4/25-gabrielle-vincent-or-monique-martin]

From Dusk Till Dawn, Season 1

Reviewed by Stephen Theaker

From Dusk Till Dawn is a television series produced and developed by Robert Rodriguez for his own El Rey network, and shown on Netflix in the UK. Unlike *Blade: The Series, Terminator: The Sarah Connor Chronicles* or *Stargate SG-1*, this isn't a sequel, it's a remake and an expansion. The outline of the plot is mostly unchanged. The Gecko brothers (nephews of Nice Guy Eddie from *Reservoir Dogs*) are bank robbers

on the run, trying to cross the border into Mexico.
They take hostages, a widowed clergyman and his two
unhappy children. They end up at a biker bar, a strip
club where the star performer is several hundred years
older than she looks. The one big difference is that
supernatural elements kick in sooner, as Richie's
visions of a mysterious woman inspire him to kill.

The cast is generally very good. D.J. Cotrona and
Zane Holtz as Seth and Richie Gecko have more time
to explore their characters and relationship than was
available to George Clooney and Quentin Tarantino,
and they use it well. Eiza Gonzalez looks the part, but
doesn't live up to Salma Hayek's star-making
performance as Santantico Pandemonium. Her
manipulations never quite ring true, though it's hard
to be menacing when you're half-undressed, as she is
in so many scenes. Wilmer Valderrama is wonderfully
serpentine as the shapeshifting vampire who
commissioned the Geckos to do the job – and
unrecognisable as adorable Fez from *That '70s Show*.
Robert Patrick (who was in the second film as a
different character) takes Harvey Keitel's role as the
grief-haunted father from the first film, and if
anything his committed performance is a step up.

Robert Rodriguez is a good fit for television. He's
made a career out of making cheap films look
expensive, and here he's making television that looks
better than most cheap films. For most of the season
this is a very good, well-made programme. It only goes
awry in the last few episodes, after everyone reaches
the vampire strip club and heads into a subterranean
magical labyrinth for a interminable wander around.
The tension disappears, characters lose their drive, and
the show falls apart, becoming very nearly
unwatchable – it's the steepest mid-season decline
since *The Twin Dilemma* followed *The Caves of
Androzani*. After the first few episodes I had liked this

so much that I thought in all seriousness a *Reservoir Dogs* television series might be a good idea. By the end, I was hoping they would stay away from *Sharkboy and Lavagirl.*

I'll certainly give season two a look – the cast are reportedly enthused about heading into uncharted territory – but it'll need to get back on track quickly or I'll be the one heading for the border.

Game of Thrones, Season 4

Reviewed by Stephen Theaker

Game of Thrones, Season 4 (Sky Atlantic/HBO) feels for a while as if it has hardly moved on from the beginning of the previous season. Jon Snow is still bumbling around beyond the wall, Sansa still wandering with the Hound, Daenarys is marching around Slavers' Bay with her army, and Joffrey is still doing bad things like the bad little king he is. The weird army we saw marching at the end of season two has yet to arrive anywhere. In television we're used to things moving rather more quickly, arcs concluding at the end of a season and new arcs beginning the season after. That doesn't really happen with *Game of Thrones*, but season three came to a famously cataclysmic conclusion, and the ripples of that final episode become tidal waves in season four. It's the aftermath of some things, the beginning of others, and there's a great big battle by the end featuring the programme's best special effects yet.

As ever with HBO, the gratuitous female nudity plays havoc with the tone, but I'm still enjoying *Game of Thrones* very much. If there's a new episode to watch, that's what we're watching. The production quality is stupendous, costumes and set design as good as any film I can think of in this genre. The cast is incredible, and always getting better. Indira Varma is a welcome addition this season, not least because this is one programme where her violent death (I assume it's coming eventually!) won't come as such a dreadful shock. Her *Torchwood* colleague Burn Gorman is almost unwatchably horrid as the leader of a gang of depraved deserters from the Black Watch. Diana Rigg joins as a schemer with a grandmotherly air, but the standout new character of the season is the Spanish-ish Viper, a dashing hedonist with a thirst for vengeance.

Westeros and the surrounding lands are a horrible place to live, even for the richest and most powerful. That absence of security, and our knowledge from previous years that any character could die at any time, makes every battle scene, every trial, every flight from danger – even every harsh glance or raised eyebrow! – a source of intense drama and excitement. It all has weight. This season lacks a bit of mystery: Bran's mystic quest for a three-eyed raven is less than intriguing, and most events and motivations are presented clearly to the viewer. But perhaps other programmes focus on secrets of the past so much because their futures are so limited, except when contracted cast members decide to leave. It's thrilling to have one programme where (unless you've read the books, and I won't until this show has finished) you really don't know what's going to happen.

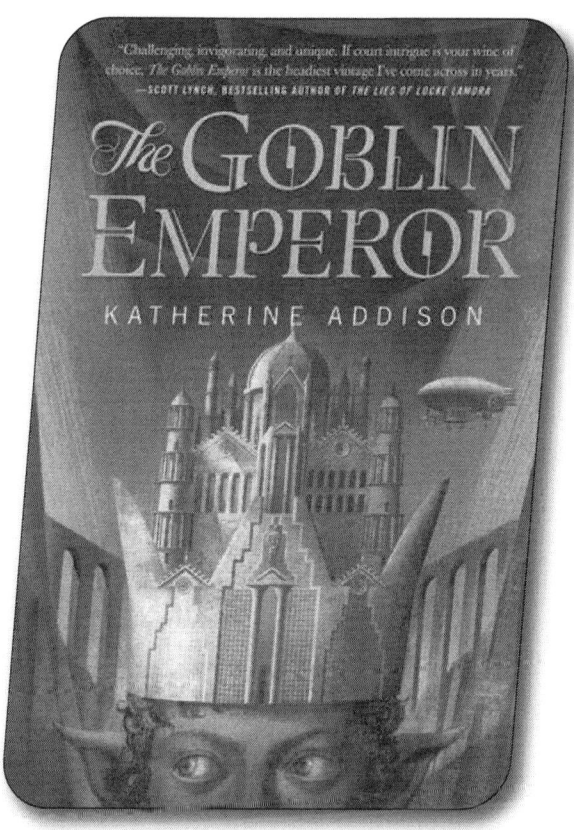

The Goblin Emperor

Reviewed by Stephen Theaker

In **The Goblin Emperor** (Tor, ebook, 6853ll)
Katherine Addison (a name which is, as the dedication
hints, a pseudonym) introduces us to Maia, an angry
young man exiled to the middle of nowhere with a
violent, oppressive guardian: his cousin Setheris. He
wakes to the news that his father and older brothers
have perished in an airship disaster, the *Wisdom of*

Choharo having crashed with no survivors on the way back from a wedding.

His deadbeat dad was Varenechibel the Fourth, 208th emperor of the Elflands. His mother, Chenelo Drazharan, was a goblin, married off to the emperor for political reasons. Maia was the accident of the marriage's single act of consummation. In looks, he takes after his mother, which would draw the distrust of the elves even if they weren't faced with him becoming their new emperor.

Anyone who has read *Claudius the God* will have an idea of what to expect next. A clever, despised protagonist, dropped into a nest of vipers, learning the ropes and coming good despite the obstacles in his way. However, this book is rather more optimistic (and isn't bound by history), and Maia – or Edrehasivar VII, as he styles himself upon becoming the 209th emperor – is lucky: in his world paying it forward pays off.

The goodwill he earns through kind words and deeds saves his life more than once – in the very first chapter he earns an essential ally through kindness to the messenger bringing word of his father's death. This is a book that moseys along in an amiable and pleasant way, with good rewarded and evil punished, and good people facing the challenge of how to stay good when dealing with bad people.

You have to root for Maia as he sorts out the mess left by his father's death, tries to reckon with his feelings about his father, and investigates whether that death was an accident or not. On top of that he must deal with plots and attempted coups, win the grudging respect of gruff bodyguards and a snooty court, negotiate with foreign powers, select a wife (and learn how to speak to her), and decide whether to build a fancy clockwork bridge.

Though there is plenty going on, it's quite a static book, Maia's new position at the heart of empire not permitting much travel. The plot progresses, on the whole, through a series of meetings and conversations. An early look at the appendices is helpful here: extracts from a handbook for travellers in the Elflands, they explain a lot about the subtle use of names and forms of address in the book.

Readers shouldn't be put off by the dialogue in the early pages – "Merciful goddesses, boy, canst do *nothing* for thyself?" cries Setheris – because it doesn't set the tone for the rest of the book. This is a good, enjoyable book, cleanly written, and though it felt quite gentle in comparison to the likes of *Game of Thrones* and is probably aimed at younger readers than me, it's nice for once to see a good person's miserable life get better rather than worse.

Godzilla

Reviewed by Stephen Theaker

By my count the new **Godzilla**, directed by Gareth
Edwards, is the twenty-third I've seen, the first being
King Kong vs Godzilla on Saturday morning television
as a child, the most recent *Godzilla, Mothra, King
Ghidorah: Giant Monsters All-Out Attack*, a week
before this new American production came out. This
is the first appearance of the monster since *Godzilla:
Final Wars*, which underperformed at the Japanese

box office but did give us the pleasure of seeing baby Godzilla ride in a truck and Roland Emmerich's female Godzilla fighting her Japanese inspiration. (It wasn't a long fight.) For the uninitiated: there are three runs of Japanese Godzilla films: the original Shōwa series, from *Godzilla* in 1954 to *Terror of Mechagodzilla* in 1975, the rebooted Heisei series, from *Godzilla 1984* through to *Godzilla vs Destroyah* in 1995, and lastly, after the America *Godzilla* of 1998 failed to produce any sequels, the Millennium series of standalone films, from *Godzilla 2000* in 1999 through to *Godzilla: Final Wars* in 2004. Most Godzilla films are entertaining (even the really bad ones, like *Godzilla vs Hedorah*), though the lack of variety does make you wonder why quite so many of them were made.

Happily, this is not another remake of the original film, nor is it yet another direct sequel. Here, the world at large is not yet aware of Godzilla's existence. Although he was sighted at sea in 1954, and attempts were made to destroy him, he hasn't previously come ashore. Rather like *Transformers: Dark of the Moon* and its explanation of the moon landings, *Godzilla* winds into itself real world events like the nuclear testing in the South Pacific, and disasters like the 2004 tsunami, the Fukushima meltdown, September 11 and the New Orleans floods are echoed throughout. Godzilla is once again a force of nature, though that hasn't always been the case in the past. In *All-Out Attack* he was supernatural, resurrected to attack Japan by the ghosts of those killed in World War II, while in other films he is a reluctant defender of the Earth against alien aggressors, or himself the servant of such aliens – he can be anything a film requires. Here he represents the power of natural forces, capable of utter destruction, yet also grace and beauty. This is his planet, really; we're the ants scurrying on its surface.

Godzilla is as powerful in this film as I've ever seen him. He has mass and strength and for once you don't have to imagine what he is like, you can see it on the screen. To take a monster represented by a man in a suit and turn that into a believable living creature, with it still being recognisably the same creature, is quite an achievement. The colossal creatures he fights are terrifyingly alien (think of that huge strange beast from the end of *The Mist*). The size and strangeness of them all is reinforced by our point of view being restricted, for most of the film, to that of the humans experiencing these events, some battles seen only through snatches of handheld camera footage on television, This is a world where humans are no longer the protagonists. We're part of the scenery, desperately trying to avoid being chewed.

Godzilla is the star, and that's reflected in the cast, made up of respected actors – Bryan Cranston, Juliette Binoche, Aaron Taylor-Johnson, Elizabeth Olsen, Ken Watanabe, Sally Hawkins – rather than the kind of movie stars who automatically make for a big opening weekends. It's a risk that pays off. They aren't superheroes, they're regular people doing their best to help others and protect their families and survive in appallingly dangerous circumstances. We spend most of the film with the military, watching their almost futile attempts to guide the creatures away from population centres, but the action begins cleverly with the workers at a nuclear plant. We've frequently seen these places destroyed by Godzilla and his fellow monsters, but to be inside the plant while such an attack is happening brings home the effect that these events have on ordinary people. It's not as if that human perspective was never represented in other Godzilla films, but it's the primary focus here.

The music reminded me in places of the Japanese scores, and that much of the story took place in Japan felt respectful to the character's origins. We often see Godzilla serenely swimming in the ocean, which seemed to reference scenes in *Godzilla vs Mothra* (1992), one of my favourite films in the series (and of all the Godzilla films I've seen, that's the one this most resembles). It's rather a dark film for much of the time, so I wish I'd watched it in 2D without the darkening effect of 3D glasses – and I would have preferred to have seen the final monster battle in daylight. But that's the worst I can find to say about it: for me this is the best Godzilla film since the Heisei era, and it's much better than the inferior films in the Shōwa series that followed 1968's excellent *Destroy All Monsters*. After some of the daft stuff past films have shown him doing, it's surprising and rather thrilling to once again be afraid of Godzilla.

Indie Cindy

Reviewed by Stephen Theaker

The return of the Pixies with **Indie Cindy** (PIAS, CD) has not been universally welcomed, coming in for particular scorn from those unhappy that Kim Deal is no longer involved. Her absence is certainly a shame, and there is a space on the album where her backing vocals should be (as there was on *Trompe Le Monde*), but it's a bit hard on the remaining members to hit them with that stick. They did wait a decade for her to agree to recording new material, and she only pulled out after the studio was booked and the gear transported to Wales. You can't blame them for pressing on in those circumstances – and I'm glad they did, because we now have a new Pixies album.

A good test of a new album by a long-established band is whether any of the songs would make it onto a

Best Of. *Indie Cindy* passes that test standing on its head: it's impossible to imagine a Best of the Pixies without "Greens and Blues", and I wouldn't be surprised to see "Snakes" and "What Goes Boom" on there either. (The latter is surely destined for a long life of soundtracking sporting montages and movie trailers.) An aspect of the band's success not often mentioned is here in spades: these songs are immense fun to sing along with! Impossible to sing "I'm the burgermeister of purgatory!" ("Indie Cindy") or "felt a burning in my solar plexus" ("Blue Eyed Hexe") or "I'm the one with all the trotters" ("Bagboy") without enjoying yourself.

My biggest grumble about the album is that it is really just a compilation of the previous EPs, or to put it another way, it's now clear the EPs were just the album doled out a bit at a time. Every song from the EPs is on here, so buying this meant buying most of the tracks a second time over (and the other three appeared on EP3, not available at first in MP3 format) – though that does make it feel like a greatest hits in itself. I hoped, and I wonder if the band hoped, that Deal might return by the album's release to add her vocals to the previously released tracks. That didn't happen, but "Bagboy" at least is a slightly different version to the original MP3 release, with the "Cover your teeth" chant coming in much later. It makes the song somewhat sleeker and meaner.

The most exciting thing about a new Pixies album having been released – apart from the existence of the album itself – is knowing that Black Francis never stops writing and recording, so there will probably be another one pretty soon. If it's as good as *Indie Cindy*, let alone better, expect lots of articles and reviews applauding their return to form, because everyone loves to tell that story. By then *Indie Cindy* will be part of the landscape, another part of the back catalogue, maybe not a *Doolittle* (how many albums are?), but certainly the peer of *Bossanova* and *Trompe Le Monde*, and maybe their better. And if the Pixies don't make another new album, at least they've said a proper goodbye: the album's last song, the jolly "Jaime Bravo", ends "Goodbye and goodnight / Goodbye".

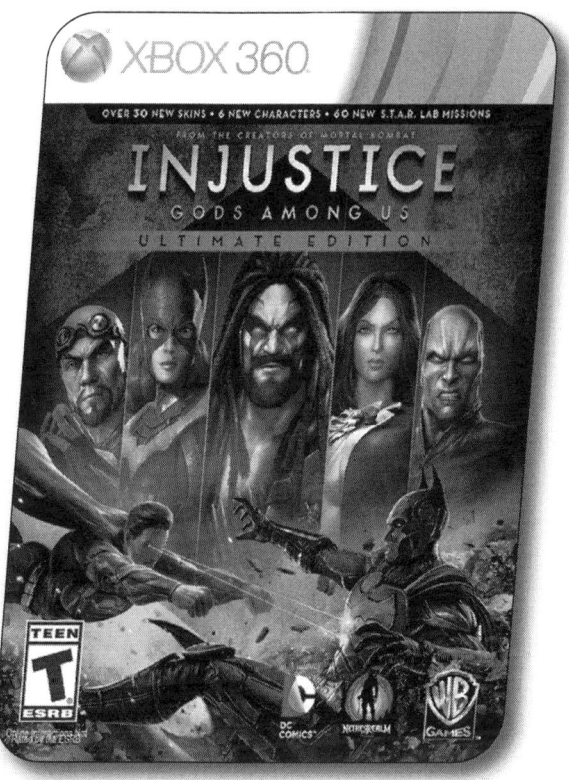

Injustice: Gods Among Us, Ultimate Edition

Reviewed by Stephen Theaker

Injustice: Gods Among Us (Xbox 360) begins in the aftermath of the nuclear destruction of Metropolis by the Joker. He's in custody, being roughed up by Batman, when Superman turns up and gets uncharacteristically rougher. Then we cut to a scene of the Justice League fighting various villains, and, if we didn't already know, we discover at last what kind of game this is: a 2D fighter, like *The Way of the Exploding Fist* without the tranquil backdrops. Each chapter of the story mode lets us fight a few bouts as a well-known character, as "our" JLA is thrown into the dark dimension that saw Metropolis's destruction, now ruled by a dictatorial Superman.

Fighting games are not usually my bag: I can't be bothered to stick with one combatant to learn all their moves, which makes for more variety in the short term but holds your skills back. *Injustice* asked way too much from my fingers – I wasn't fast enough to pull off many of the special moves – but button mashing produces entertaining results. The main appeal of this game for me was in the variety of DC characters involved, including a decent selection of female heroes and villains. It is always pleasant to see Green Lantern pound Doomsday with a giant green hammer, and to be at the controls when it happens.

Drawing on the DLC that followed the original game, this Ultimate Edition adds six characters to the roster: Lobo, Batgirl, General Zod, Martian Manhunter, Zatanna and *Mortal Kombat*'s Scorpion (I think *Injustice* is built on the architecture of the recent *MK* revamp). It also includes lots of special missions – mini-games in which you have to pull off certain moves or achieve special objectives, like blasting asteroids or winning a battle without being hit – and many extra skins, based on classic stories like *Superman: Red Son* and *The Killing Joke*.

It's everything I wanted from a DC universe fighting game, and as well as being a good game it tells a good story, as reflected perhaps in the success of the tie-in comics. The return of voice actors from the DC animated universe was a treat, and though I generally skip cut scenes, those here are well done. It seems daft at first to see Harley Quinn fight Doomsday without being instantly killed, but this is explained in the story mode: a gift of super-strength and invulnerability from the evil Superman to his lieutenants, now also in the hands of the rebels and villains. Local multiplayer works well, allowing logged-in players to swap in and out with no problems. It's all good fun. Grim, dark fun.

Maleficent

Reviewed by Douglas J. Ogurek

Mistress of All Evil repackaged as multidimensional heroine.

Excepting the horror genre, not many films are named after a villain. Villainesses are even rarer. Moreover, it's hard to find a fully developed hero in a contemporary special effects-heavy blockbuster.

Maleficent (2014), directed by Robert Stromberg, fills these gaps exquisitely by recasting the iconic

Mistress of All Evil as a fairy born into a privileged, human-free life of gallivanting amid an idyllic forest filled with magical inhabitants. Then she meets the boy Stefan, who ultimately betrays her to assume the throne. Jilted lover Maleficent slaps a curse on King Stefan's daughter: before her sixteenth birthday, Aurora will prick her finger on a spinning wheel needle and fall into an eternal sleep, unless awakened by true love's kiss.

The king orders the elimination of all spinning wheels and dispatches his daughter to a remote cottage, where Maleficent immediately finds her.

The majority of the film juxtaposes King Stefan's self-destructive search for the evasive "villainess" and Maleficent's relationship with the unsuspecting Aurora.

Initially, the film seems to move toward an eco-tale in the vein of *Avatar* (2009) when the child Maleficent chides a human intruder for stealing a precious stone from her forest. However, *Maleficent* veers from this direction and instead focuses on an unlikely relationship between a Goody Two-shoes and a shadowy sorceress. The film offers a moving, if predictable climax and healthy doses of what the best fairy tales deliver: justice and triumph.

A Jolie Good Performance

Having borne Charlize Theron's overly dramatic portrayal of Queen Ravenna in *Snow White and the Huntsman* (2012) – the actress made the most of a poorly scripted character – I was concerned that Angelina Jolie's Maleficent would follow in her footsteps. Fortunately, Jolie, armed with those unmistakable horns and some vicious cheekbones, rises to the occasion.

There are times when Jolie rages. When Maleficent discovers that she has been betrayed, for instance, she conveys first shock with her quiet realization, then shrieking outrage. Fortunately, she avoids the Hollywood cliché of extending her arms and screaming at the sky.

But what truly makes Jolie's performance a pleasure to watch are her moments of restraint. When Maleficent tells Aurora that "there is evil in this world, hatred and revenge", one senses both forced constraint and self-castigation in her tone. When people speak to her, Maleficent may stare at them for a couple seconds before responding. Her reserved nature, coupled with her economy of movement and rigid posture, rebels against a real world that never stops talking and moving.

In one of the most endearing scenes, a mud fight breaks out between Aurora and the forest creatures. When a stray splotch of mud hits Maleficent, the revellers look worried and quiet pervades the scene, with one exception: Diaval, Maleficent's shapeshifting henchman, bursts into laughter. A torrent of mud slams him in the face and as the laughing resumes, Maleficent smiles... slightly.

Go Forth Fearlessly

Disney's revamp of the villainess joins other blockbusters like the *The Hunger Games* and *Divergent* series in the ongoing dialogue about the role of contemporary women both within and beyond the silver screen.

Once, the childless recluse with an unorthodox sense of fashion was restricted to desolate outposts and gloomy alcoves. Now Maleficent has stepped out unabashed. There is something liberating about plopping a gaunt-faced villainess in flowing black robes into a sunny, verdant landscape where a blonde frolics.

"I am not afraid," Maleficent tells Aurora, who

embodies the old-fashioned notion of what a woman should be. Maybe, *Maleficent* hints, a woman's success lies not in being whisked away or saved by a man, but rather in her own ingenuity. Maybe they should have named this film *Femaleficent*.

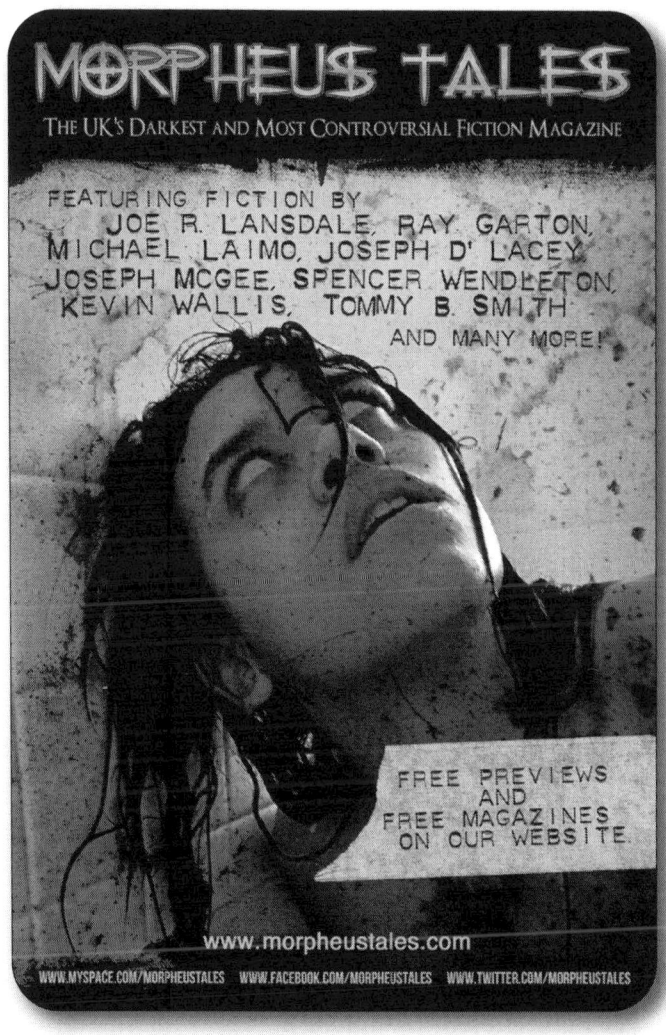

The Professor and the Siren

Reviewed by Stephen Theaker

The Professor and the Siren (New York Review Books, 78pp) is a new translation by Stephen Twilley of three stories by Giuseppe Tomasi Di Lampedusa, all of which originally appeared in the 1961 collection *I racconti*. The book will also include an introduction by Marina Warner (not available for review).

The first and longest is the thirty-eight-page title story, "The Professor and the Siren", in its Italian publication "La Sirena" (the title change is perhaps to distinguish this volume from others), about an elderly professor who reminisces fondly about his sexual encounter, at the age of twenty-four, with a mermaid who had "the smooth face of a sixteen-year-old", an "adolescent" with "features of infantile purity" and "decidedly youthful sensuality".

She's much older than she looks, being in fact Lighea, daughter of Calliope, and she helps his career immensely by giving him the unique opportunity to converse in ancient Greek: he is now "the most illustrious Hellenist of our time" – but that doesn't stop the story feeling rather grotty.

"And were you all not disgusted," the professor says to our narrator about his own pair of lovers – that is, adult, human, women – "they as much as you, you as much as they – to kiss and cuddle your future carcasses between evil-smelling sheets?"

To finish the story one must also get past the descriptions of this lovely old gentleman spitting onto the floor of the café on Via Po! The narrator finds this much more off-putting than the description of the mermaid, but relents when his friend explains that the spitting is for show, and the emissions that hit the floor contain no catarrh and very little saliva. Delightful.

The other two stories feature no fantasy elements, but are more likeable. In "Joy and the Law" ("La Gioia e la legge") a downtrodden office worker wins a fifteen-pound panettone – he was voted the most deserving employee by his charitable colleagues. But his hopes of enjoying this uncommon treat fall prey to existing social obligations. "The Blind Kittens" ("I gattini ciechi") tells of Don Batassano Ibba, and the legends that have grown up around him as his property empire expands across Sicily.

Though issues with sex and spitting spoilt the first story for me, two of the three were good, the translation reads elegantly, and their portrayal of a particular time and place feels authentic, whether it is or not. It's probably not a book many of our readers will rush out to buy, and there are other translations available, but I found at least some things to enjoy in it and you may too.

Sabrina the Teenage Witch: 50 Magical Stories

Reviewed by Stephen Theaker

Sabrina the Teenage Witch: 50 Magical Stories
(Archie, ebook, 349pp) provides a cheap,
comprehensive introduction to one of Archie's most
famous characters, a peppy teenage witch who, much
as she did in the successful television series, usually

lives with her aunts, Hilda and Zelda, and their talking cat Salem. Salem is an uncle who tried to conquer the world (or, in other stories, broke off his engagement with the head witch) and felinisation was his punishment. Sabrina is a good-hearted girl, but isn't above using her powers selfishly. She's usually an agent of karma (turning chauvinists into pigs, for example), at other times its victim.

One problem with the book is that it zags around from one period to another of the comic without a nod to continuity, which will presumably baffle readers who haven't had the benefit of reading an overview of the series (like the one in *Slings and Arrows).* In one strip Sabrina's aunts are green-skinned hags, in another human-looking and pretty, so dateable they end up double-booked. In one strip Sabrina's dating Harvey and going to school in Riverdale with Archie, Betty and Veronica, in the next she's at a monster school, her boyfriend is a vampire, and her best friends are an invisible girl (Cleara!) and a genuinely disconcertingly eyeball-headed girl (Eyeda!). The very first story says Sabrina mustn't fall in love or she'll lose all her powers and become human, and in the second she's smooching Harvey on the sofa.

I've read a lot of Archie comics on Comixology over the last couple of years. A lot. For one thing they're cheap and plentiful, which is how I like my comics. (Compare with DC, who not so long ago had only single issues on Comixology, and Marvel whose Comixology collections are often extremely expensive.) And they are ideally suited to digital reading. The lovely bright colours look wonderful on digital displays, and the simple layouts and square panels work perfectly in Guided View on any device. Almost any given panel of an Archie book looks like a pop art masterpiece when zoomed to fit an iPad screen.

But this Sabrina collection was not my favourite of

them, and my daughters didn't find it as appealing as I expected either (they adored other digital collections such as *Betty's Story Time* and *The Archie Wedding*, and have become much bigger fans of the Josie and the Pussycats movie since realising that it's part of this comics world). The stories here are readable enough, and there are a lot of them, but Sabrina in these comics just doesn't have the zip that Melissa Joan Hart gave her on television. She lacks any strong personality traits – unless being able to cast spells counts as one – and she doesn't face any real challenges in the stories.

If you're looking for an Archie comic to hook children into reading, go for Betty, Veronica or Jughead instead.

Star Wars: Maul – Lockdown

Reviewed by Jacob Edwards

Blowing the horns of dilemma.

When the first *Star Wars* prequel, *A Phantom Menace*, was unveiled with grandiose, heraldic fanfare across cinema screens in 1999, the lightsaber thrum of expectation was always likely to sputter and fizzle. Disappointed, we were, and not just with Jar Jar Binks. There was also Darth Maul: the red-skinned, horned and tattooed, mad-eyed, devil-modelled Sith Lord, whose agility and snarling savagery promised a danger no less than that of the dark, prowling power of Vader, but whose ultimate delivery – standing *non compos mentis* while an erstwhile-dangling Obi-Wan springs up and out of the reactor shaft, force-grabs Qui-Gon Jinn's lightsaber, somersaults over Maul's head and cuts him in half – proved utterly, almost insultingly flaccid. This was someone with the Force aptitude to wield a double-bladed lightsaber and take on two Jedi simultaneously. To die with such ineptness... It was a dramatic let-down, the emotionally hollow like of which could only be achieved by such clumsy scripting as having Obi-Wan Kenobi, rather than allowing Darth Vader to strike him down in *A New Hope*, instead merely tripping on his own robes and accidentally impaling himself on Vader's lightsaber. To have Maul dispatched in so undignified a manner was to reduce a martial virtuoso to the level of an extra from Japanese fight-fantasy *Monkey*, and pratfalling along with him went any aspirations the prequelogy might have harboured to match strokes with the original *Star Wars* saga.

Vale, Darth Maul. the true phantom menace of the film.

Carrying this perspective fifteen years into the future, the more casual *Star Wars* fan could be excused for greeting Joe Schreiber's latest book with a Binksian droop of scepticism and ambivalence. **Maul: Lockdown** (Century) is set pre-prequelogy and in the main features no familiar characters other than Maul himself, with only fleeting appearances by Jabba the Hutt and a nascent Darth Sidious. The story takes place in a diabolical prison, to which Maul has been sent to track down a spectral arms dealer, and begins with a six-page fight to the death that blends horror motifs with comic book sensibility. These two elements interplay throughout the novel, and as each short chapter unfolds and Schreiber demonstrates himself to be neither squeamish nor overly concerned to remove action scenes from their still-frames (indeed, one particularly casual sequence jump on page 128 sees Maul, who is under a moratorium on Force use, physically grab hold of a Chandra-Fan who just previously had scuttled up a ladder and thus was nowhere near him), those of us whose readership is grounded in the big-screen revelations of 1977 will quickly realise that Schreiber's manifestation of *Star Wars* is not the rousing space opera that we signed up for. Sweeping, swashbuckling and fanciful are set aside in favour of confined, gruesome and humourless. In fact, with an amoral protagonist pitted against foes who remain almost entirely unmitigated in their respective evils, *Maul: Lockdown* could well be repudiated as holding no substantial connection to the *Star Wars* canon. As the publishing industry continues to spawn its offshoots, George Lucas's vision seems to be receding into the long time ago and the achingly far away. This is not *Star Wars* at all. It's the garbage compactor of *A New Hope* magnified beyond all proportions and left to its own dark devices.

Divorced from its origins, it's also rather good.

Maul: Lockdown is built around a seemingly unpromising premise, and is made by both cover and blurb to seem literature-poor and pulpy. Schreiber, however, though unashamedly engaging the comic book action/horror hyperdrive, transcends this red-blurred veneer and delivers a surprisingly substantial payload. His prison setting is far from typical – a Rubik's penitentiary in space, its design constantly subject to reconfiguration – and the inmates are free to wander the complex, limited only by failsafes implanted in their hearts and an obligation (thus warranted) to return to their cells for televised death matches: grist to the mill for the prison warden and the gambling underworld. This floating pocket of the *Star Wars* universe is depraved and grotesque yet suitably fleshed out, the *dramatis personae* falling within a broadly malevolent swathe but given sufficient individuality both to defy stereotype and to foster genuine intrigue. Schreiber writes in a series of vignettes – 76 chapters squeezed into 330 pages; caged restlessness giving way to pent-up release – yet the story builds across three broad acts and the overall pacing conveys something not unlike that hallmark epic quality, manifest throughout *A New Hope*, *The Empire Strikes Back* and *Return of the Jedi*, that might well be thought lacking in many of the freestanding *Star Wars* novels, and indeed in the prequelogy arc spanning *The Phantom Menace*, *Attack of the Clones* and *Revenge of the Sith*. Schreiber also deserves credit for successfully presenting an antihero, allowing the reader to engage with Maul's ignoble mission while remaining unsympathetic to him within a broader *Star Wars* context. Maul is relentless, and though his deadly prowess – which is to the fore, even sans any recourse to the Force – does give rise to the unfortunate side-effect of accentuating the limpness of his demise in *The Phantom Menace*, his developing backstory in *Lockdown* is at least representative of the formidable figure we see up to that point. The character lacks depth and is inherently odious, but the same could be said of Anakin Skywalker as he goes through his contrived metamorphosis to become Darth Vader. Schreiber's portrayal of Maul was the more difficult task, and though the reading is not always pleasant, we should take some grim satisfaction that as warden of the dark side he has kept his charge believable and consistent.

Second time around the trilogy bush, that's more than George Lucas managed.

The Strange Talent of Luther Strode

Reviewed by Stephen Theaker

You would be forgiven for thinking that **The Strange Talent of Luther Strode** (Image, tpb, 162pp) must be related to getting himself published despite the poorness of his book. As well as his megamuscles and talent for ultraviolence, he must be extremely persuasive. Either that or writer Justin Jordan and artist Tradd Moore know where the Image Comics skeletons are kept.

As the book begins, Luther has just been shot seven times in the chest, but he's caught the bullets in his muscles, and works out how to push them back out. He's also just killed half a dozen guys by kicking and punching them so hard they exploded. And he's got X-ray vision, which helps when he's looking for weak spots.

Rewind to find out how he got those powers: he was a skinny guy getting bullied, who sent off for *The Hercules Method* – though it turns out there is a bit more to it than that. He gets into trouble as bad guys come after him, does some fights, gets cosy with a sassy girl, tries to keep his mum and best pal out of trouble.

This was one of the worst comic books I've read in recent years. There is some fighting, and anger, and violence – lots of blood and rage – and if that's what you're after, you might go for it. The story was poor, and the artwork isn't that appealing, unless you really love seeing what people's muscles look like under the skin.

It grabs bits from *Spider-Man* – Luther puts his Flash Thompson in a neck brace – and *Flex Mentallo*, mixes it with Garth Ennis levels of blood, but lacks any of that writer's wit or imagination. Best avoided. The basic idea of a weed becoming a strongman was handled more imaginatively in *Major Bummer* (reviewed in #38).

In one set of panels a gun is fired at the main villain and he dodges it, but he also, between the bullet being fired and it reaching him, manages to say, "Ah, well then..." – which makes no sense, unless he was talking so quickly the person he was talking to wouldn't have been able to understand him. Like the book itself, it's supposed to look cool but falls hopelessly flat.

The Tripods

Reviewed by Jacob Edwards

Challenging the rule of three.

When setting out to make **The Tripods** for BBC TV, producer Richard Bates faced the daunting prospect of having his work judged against two veritable institutions. Firstly, there was the source material: the critically and popularly acclaimed trilogy of books by John Christopher (the SF pen name of prolific author Sam Youd). Secondly, there was *Doctor Who*, in whose traditional Saturday evening timeslot *The Tripods* was to be broadcast, and against whose ailing ratings it would be measured as a successful (or otherwise) purveyor of children's SF drama. Working in Bates's favour was, of course, the strength of Youd's post-apocalyptic, historically regressed invasion-cum-resistance adventure narrative, but also a budget of unprecedented splendour and the opportunity to shoot on location across England, Wales and Switzerland. Composer Ken Freeman – who'd previously played keyboards on Jeff Wayne's musical interpretation of *The War of the Worlds* – synthesised a classic score full of portent and menace. Veteran *Doctor Who* director Christopher Barry was brought in to direct. The battle lines were set.

> "This was when Richard Bates was making *The Tripods*. He scrupulously sent advance scripts and asked for comments and thanked me for them, but took no notice." – Sam Youd, interviewed by Colin Brockhurst in 2009.

Series 1 of *The Tripods* comprises 13 half-hour episodes (although these appear to have been edited down to 25 minutes for commercial broadcast and, frustratingly, at least some editions of the DVD), and follows *The White Mountains*, which is the first book of Youd's trilogy. Screenwriter Alick Rowe clearly set out to closely capture the spirit and much of the detail of the original book, and at first any deviations reflect merely the disparity that necessarily must exist between a written first-person narrative and a more visual depiction of context and conflict. That the adaptation becomes looser as the series progresses can largely be explained (and was, by Bates to Youd) as a different sort of necessity: that of having used up the allotted portion of location work and thus having to extemporise new material for a studio setting. Despite any affront this might have caused to those who read first and watched second, the narrative and its realisation remain compelling. The eponymous tripods are used sparingly, but to good purpose, and where *The Tripods* overtly broke from *Doctor Who*'s mould in allocating more of its budget towards realistic settings and effects than towards a high-profile principal and guest cast, nevertheless the acting stands up. The three main characters (Will, Henry and Beanpole) are adolescents, and the actors (John Shackley, Jim Baker and Ceri Seel), though largely inexperienced, were rigorously auditioned – there were 400 applicants for the role of Will – and play well off each other in carrying the story forward. (Many viewers today would be genuinely surprised to learn that none of the three went on to establish an acting career subsequent to *The Tripods*.) The cliff-hangers are less forced and certainly no less effective than the pantomimic "end of episode" howlers that seemed *de rigueur* of John Nathan-Turner's *Doctor Who* at the time, and perhaps the worst criticism that can be made of the first series of *The Tripods* is that some of its more extreme moments of character imperilment are, upon resumption, glossed over with little or even no explanation proffered. Notwithstanding such liberties, the production as a whole succeeds admirably in portraying both the subjugation of mankind and the three boys' at times harrowing quest to find the free men living in the white mountains. *The Tripods* averaged somewhere in the vicinity of 6.3 million viewers across the 13 episodes of its lustrous debut. A month later *Doctor Who* returned to Saturday evenings after its dalliance with midweek broadcasts, and in comparison averaged 7.1 million for the season.

"After the reasonably faithful book-replication at the beginning, I was probably bound to find the increasingly wide divergences irritating. My guess was that someone thought he could improve things by following a more orthodox science-fiction path. ... I just thought it silly. The second series got so far off my path that I just couldn't recognise it." – Sam Youd, *ibid*.

Series 2 of *The Tripods* comprises 12 half-hour (or 25-minute) episodes, and ostensibly is based on *The City of Gold and Lead* – the second book of Youd's trilogy, in which Will and newcomer Fritz (Robin Hayter) infiltrate one of the tripods' cities and encounter the beings who have enslaved mankind. The acting remains very good, as do the special effects in fashioning an alien environment that successfully walks a tightrope between the bedazzlingly futuristic and the fuzzy electrobuzz of Plastic Bertrand's music video for *Ça Plane Pour Moi*. The story adaptation, however, in the second series comes not from Alick Rowe but rather courtesy of Christopher Penfold, who had made numerous contributions to *Space: 1999* and seems to have taken this as some sort of creative licence to senselessly pervert Youd's original work. With no obvious impetus for doing so, Penfold cuts the casual brutality of the alien masters and pastes it (along with a recurring, fetishist riff) onto privileged macho men guards whose function is inexplicable within the world setting and who present more as a sadistic clique of collaborationists than the docile, mind-controlled slaves of the book. By spurning not just the physical but also the textual gravity of Youd's scenario, Penfold strips the series of much of its narrative weight, thereby rendering *The Tripods* in much the same faux dark, yet garish and rather discordant shades that ran through mid-eighties *Who*. Considered as an unfolding adventure, series two of *The Tripods* still holds the viewer's attention, but there are jarring ups and downs, and by the point where Penfold has invested his version of the city of gold and lead with a kitsch synth-sleaze nightclub and a wholly manufactured, manifestly unnecessary second race of alien beings, audience figures were starting to drop, averaging out at 5.1 million across the twelve episodes. This, as it turned out, was more than the next season of *Doctor Who* would manage (4.8 million), but it was at best a Pyrrhic victory. Michael Grade (then controller of BBC1) had little time for SF that didn't pull its weight, and so *Doctor Who* was sent into hiatus, Colin Baker uttering the bitter parting words "Carrot juice, carrot juice, carrot juice". *The Tripods* was axed altogether, and what had been intended as an *Empire Strikes Back*-style purgatorial ending that would leave people pining for the third series ("Has it all been for nothing?" Will laments), turned out to be the proverbial it: a most sombre and unsatisfying conclusion indeed.

Never repeated by the BBC, yet fondly remembered and in sufficient demand as to be released 25 years later on DVD, *The Tripods* remains an engrossing SF adventure drama that will appeal to today's young adult audience every bit as much as it did to that of the mid-1980s. Though relatively sedate in terms of plot, none of the episodes *feel* slow-moving. In fact, viewers may well find themselves swept along, watching several instalments at a time and caught up in events until the bad penny drops and suddenly, confoundingly, the adventure is cut short. It is impossible now to say whether the unmade third series would have done justice to *The Pool of Fire* – the concluding book, in which Will, Henry, Beanpole and Fritz head a last-ditch attack to overthrow the masters and save the Earth from the deadly terraforming that has been planned. It could perhaps have been as rousing and poignant as Youd's own dénouement. In the wrong hands it could have been a fiasco. Without the act of observation, we'll never know; but if the series' cancellation hangs dourly over television history, clouding our appreciation of the BBC, at least in this instance there is a silver lining: very few people who watch *The Tripods* will be content to finish off where Michael Grade drew his bottom line; many will turn to the novels, and in doing so will come to know Sam Youd's enthralling trilogy (plus prequel) in its written form, and also, hopefully, the wider canon of his John Christopher output and thence the enduring lure of imaginative and well-crafted science fiction.

DVD release: 23/9/2009 (2|entertain / BBC Worldwide). Original broadcast: 15/9/1984 – 8/12/1984 (Series 1); 7/9/1985 – 23/11/1985 (Series 2).

True Detective, Season 1

Reviewed by Stephen Theaker

Is **True Detective, Season 1** (Sky Atlantic, TV, 8 episodes) a crime programme or a supernatural programme? Even by the end I wasn't entirely sure, though I suppose the title is a clue. I'll hedge my bets and call it horror.

The series tells the story of two police officers in Louisiana working together for the first time. Marty Hart (Woody Harrelson) is a family man cheating on his wife (Michelle Monaghan). Rust Cohle, played by an incandescent Matthew McConaughey, is a loner with a bare apartment who cribs his bleak philosophy of life from the likes of Thomas Ligotti. They don't get on – a shame given how much time they'll spend stuck in a car together.

They catch a disturbing homicide, a young woman posed nude by a tree in the middle of a field with a crown of antlers. Investigations reveal she was a girl who went missing a long time ago, and soon Marty and Rust are falling into a rabbit hole of abducted children, cover-ups, abandoned schools and churches, secret societies and conspiracies. That's all happening in the mid-nineties, but their investigation is framed by interviews in 2012 with a portly Marty and an unhinged Rust.

Both lead actors give what I'd be tempted to call career best performances, if I ignored how many of their performances I haven't yet seen. Marty is funny when getting riled by Rust, but behaves like an utter jerk towards his wife, and worse towards his girlfriend. Woody Harrelson makes every cruel comment feel in character, never holding back to preserve a good-guy image. Marty's ruining his own life, and he knows it.

McConaughey deserves all the awards that don't go to Harrelson. He (with help from the costume, make-up and hair departments, of course) creates a stunning contrast between the handsome young Rust, looking like he stepped out of a Paul Grist comic, just about keeping it together despite a miserable spell undercover for the DEA, and the dishevelled, ruined guy he becomes – but you never doubt that it's the same guy.

Though the programme comes close to perfection, it doesn't quite get there. The exploitative female nudity in some episodes is crass and embarrassing, as sexy as the contractual obligation to HBO one suspects it to have been. The final episode doesn't quite live up to the heights that precede it, and features a cringeworthy spiritual discussion that felt shoehorned in to satisfy the needs of the actor who delivers it.

But step over those things and you'll find a stunning piece of work. Nic Pizzolatto writes all eight episodes, and Cary Joji Fukunaga directs them all, which gives it, whether in quiet reflection or thrilling action, an unusual degree of creative consistency – though of course that's only a good thing because it's consistently excellent. I'd call it an eight-hour film, but this is television so compelling it puts cinema to shame.

The assumption seems to be that season two will feature a new pair of detectives. If that's been confirmed offscreen, it seems a shame. Rust and Marty worked together for several years, and for many of those they thought this case was over. What else did they investigate in that time? And what happens next? I would love to find out.

La Vallée Infernale

Read by Stephen Theaker

La Vallée Infernale (in *Tout Bob Morane 1*, Les Éditions Ananké, ebook, 10,308ll) by Henri Vernes is the first novel in the long-running Bob Morane series, which doesn't seem to have made much of an impact in Anglophone countries. Post-WWII Bob is working as a courier pilot for a shifty operator who has him run some scallywags to Papua New Guinea.

It's supposed to be an flyover, but upon arrival they demand to land, and when Bob declines they force a crash, into an area cut off by mountains, ruled by dangerous tribes, and far from safety. His honour forces Bob to attempt the protection of the idiots who have landed him in the mess.

But what to do when they announce their intention to steal the emerald eyes of a statue worshipped by a nearby tribe? And what of their willingness to slay the entire tribe by machine gun should it be necessary? Bob's only friends in this situation are his two firm fists and his loyal Scottish chum. The chances of them escaping intact seem desperately slim.

It's appropriate to describe this as a reading of *La Vallée Infernale* rather than a review, because, as usual, having read a book in the original French I can never be sure how well I've understood it. (It's hard enough understanding the books I've read in English!) For example, in this novel I read the following: "Morane tendait le bras vers les deux prisonniers entravés à leurs poteaux, de chaque côté de l'idole".

I took that to mean "Morane held out an arm towards the two prisoners boiling in their pots, on either side of the idol", and immediately sprang to Twitter to decry the book's old-fashioned racism. In fact, "poteaux" means "posts", and "entravés" means "chained". Now, in that case it's not as if I grossly misjudged the book – the men *were* still going to be eaten by cannibals with bones through their noses! But the potential for such tiny mistranslations to be scattered through the whole book would make a review unfair.

What I adore about Bob Morane is that he is no rock. He is a tough fighter, of course, but he is prey to crippling fear and doubts, an existentialist action hero. A typical passage reads: "Une sueur glacée noyait son front, tandis qu'il se répétait en lui-même: 'Tu dois réussir, Bob. Il faut que tu réussisses!'" (An icy sweat drowned his brow, while he repeated to himself, "You must succeed, Bob. You must!")

One thing that puzzled me about this novel was why Bob let his villain escape so often. He knows the guy's after the emerald eyes of the idol, he knows that he's ready to kill men, women and children to get it, and yet Bob lets him stroll around free as a bird.

I enjoyed this novel immensely, despite its dated elements, because Bob himself is such an interesting character. He's been a huge influence on my little-read

Howard Phillips series of stories, where I try to put a hero with similarly overdeveloped sensibilities into traditional action hero situations. With the series of Bob Morane omnibus editions now available as ebooks – and included in the Kindle lending library – I'm sure it won't be the last of the series I read.

Also Received, But Not Yet Reviewed

Notes by Stephen Theaker

Beal, Cliffort, *The Raven's Banquet* (Solaris)

Bialer, Matt, *Tell Them What I Saw* (PS Publishing):
poetry from the Stanza imprint

Brown, Eric, *Famadihana on Fomalhaut IV* (PS
Publishing)

Buckell, Tobias S., *Hurricane Fever* (Del Rey): taking
up the story of an interesting character from *Arctic
Rising*, which was reviewed in #45

Cawkwell, Sarah, *Heirs of the Demon King: Uprising*
(Solaris)

Cooper, James, *Strange Fruit* (PS Publishing)

Crowther, Peter, and Nick Gevers (eds), *Memoryville
Blues* (PS Publishing)

Hurley, Kameron, *Infidel* (Del Rey)

Jasienski, Bruno, *The Legs of Izoloa Morgan* (Twisted
Spoon Press)

Joshi, S.T. (ed.), *Black Wings III* (PS Publishing)

Lanagan, Margo, *We Three Kids* (PS Publishing)

Levé, Edouard, *Works* (Dalkey Archive Press)

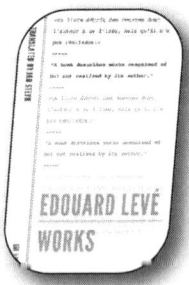 

Levene, Rebecca, *Smiler's Fair* (Hodder & Stoughton):
I've ended up reviewing this for *Interzone*, but we'll
run the review on our blog next year when I break
for NaNoWriMo

Lovecraft, H.P., *The Dream-Quest of Unknown Kadath*
(PS Publishing): illustrated by Pete Von Sholly

Lovecraft, H.P., *The Dreams in the Witch House* (PS Publishing): part of the Lovecraft Illustrated series

Lovecraft, H.P., *The Dunwich Horror* (PS Publishing)

Lovegrove, James, *World of Fire* (Solaris)

Mamatas, Nick, *The Last Weekend* (PS Publishing)

Matheson, Richard Christian, *The Ritual of Illusion* (PS Publishing)

Richards, Justin, Mark Morris, George Mann and Paul Finch, *Doctor Who: Tales of Trenzalore* (BBC Books)

Shields, Jim, *Baby Strange* (PS Publishing)

Stenson, Peter, *Fiend* (Windmill Books)

Strahan, Jonathan (ed.), *Reach for Infinity* (Rebellion Publishing): anthology including original fiction from Alastair Reynolds, Aliette de Bodard, Ian McDonald, Pat Cadigan, Hannu Rajaniemi and Kathleen Ann Goonan

Various, *2000 AD Sci-Fi Special* (Rebellion Publishing): *2000AD* have also been sending us individual issues in pdf of their excellent comic, which we haven't listed here

Wagner, John, Michael Carroll, Rob Williams, Trevor Hairsine, Ben Willsher, PJ Holden, *Judge Dredd: Day of Chaos: Fallout* (2000 AD Graphic Novels)

Watson, Ian, *The Best of Ian Watson* (PS Publishing)

Watson, Ian, *The Uncollected Ian Watson* (PS Publishing)

Forthcoming Attractions

Expect **Theaker's Quarterly Fiction #49** at the end of September 2014. Deadline for submissions is **31 August 2014**.

(The deadline is a bit short because this issue's a month late: we gave the wrong deadline on the blog and decided to stick with it.)

We are also looking ahead to **Theaker's Quarterly Fiction #50**, due out at Christmas, with a copy deadline of November 31. We're hoping to make this one a celebration of all that's gone before, so we'd love to hear from past contributors.

Most weeks begin with a new review on our blog: **www.theakersquarterly.blogspot.com**

Stephen tweets with barely hidden malevolence at: **www.twitter.com/Rolnikov**

Our email address is: **theakersquarterlyfiction@gmail.com**

Printed in Great Britain
by Amazon.co.uk, Ltd.,
Marston Gate.